Two Tails Animal Refuge

A second chance at life and love!

Welcome to Two Tails Animal Refuge in Australia's beautiful Blue Mountains! Vets Hazel and Kiara have one goal: to rescue and rehome vulnerable animals. The refuge staff work around the clock. So there's no time for Hazel and Kiara to think about love. Until a vet and a surgeon lead them to ask, "Is it time for my happily-ever-after?"

The Vet's Unexpected Family
By Alison Roberts

When a baby is abandoned at vet Hazel Davidson's Cogee Beach clinic, she's stunned to discover the newborn has been left in the care of her colleague Finn! The pair pull together to care for the baby, but could they become a real family?

A Rescue Dog to Heal Them
By Marion Lennox

All vet Kiara wants is enough money to keep her beloved Two Tails Animal Refuge afloat. But when she is paid to find a suitable rescue dog and help settle him with his new family, Kiara realizes she might have bitten off more than she can chew!

Dear Reader,

When we lost our beloved dog Mitzi, my husband and I visited an animal shelter—just to see. There we fell in love with a half border collie, half dachshund. The shelter staff told us he might have future problems with his back, so we thought we'd ring a vet friend and do some research before deciding. Big mistake. Go for it, our friend vet said, but by the time we got back someone else had adopted our boofy, sausage-dog-type mate. We now have Rusty, who we adore, but part of us still regrets that stubby, elongated body, those big brown eyes and floppy ears, and that very wiggly tail.

I've always had the greatest admiration for the work animal shelters do, and with our Two Tails duo, my cowriter, Alison Roberts, and I have tried to give you a glimpse of the work behind the scenes. Kiara and Hazel have found their happily-ever-after in this duo, and we hope you can find lots of happy moments while you read them, too.

Marion Lennox

A RESCUE DOG TO HEAL THEM

MARION LENNOX

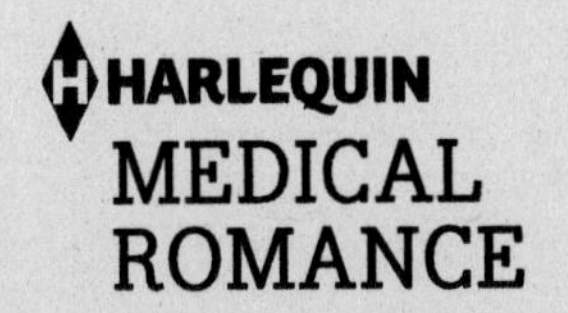

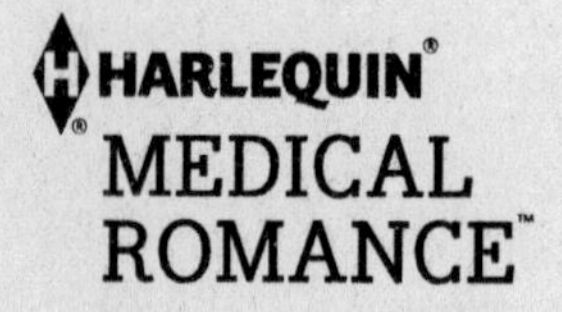

Recycling programs for this product may not exist in your area.

ISBN-13: 978-1-335-40912-6

A Rescue Dog to Heal Them

This is a work of fiction. Names, characters, places and incidents are either the product of the author's imagination or are used fictitiously. Any resemblance to actual persons, living or dead, businesses, companies, events or locales is entirely coincidental.

This edition published by arrangement with Harlequin Books S.A.

For questions and comments about the quality of this book, please contact us at CustomerService@Harlequin.com.

Harlequin Enterprises ULC
22 Adelaide St. West, 41st Floor
Toronto, Ontario M5H 4E3, Canada
www.Harlequin.com

Printed in U.S.A.

Marion Lennox has written over one hundred romance novels and is published in over one hundred countries and thirty languages. Her international awards include the prestigious RITA® award (twice!) and the *RT Book Reviews* Career Achievement Award for "a body of work which makes us laugh and teaches us about love." Marion adores her family, her kayak, her dog and lying on the beach with a book someone else has written. Heaven!

Books by Marion Lennox

Harlequin Medical Romance

Bondi Bay Heroes

Finding His Wife, Finding a Son

The Baby They Longed For
Second Chance with Her Island Doc
Rescued by the Single Dad Doc
Pregnant Midwife on His Doorstep
Mistletoe Kiss with the Heart Doctor
Falling for His Island Nurse
Healing Her Brooding Island Hero

Harlequin Romance

English Lord on Her Doorstep
Cinderella and the Billionaire

Visit the Author Profile page
at Harlequin.com for more titles.

This duo marks Alison Roberts's one hundredth book. I've loved Alison's beautifully researched, exciting, passionate, emotional reads since I picked up her first, and for many years now I've now been privileged to call her my friend. Congratulations, Alison! Here's to friendship, and to many, many more wonderful romances.

Praise for Marion Lennox

"What an entertaining, fast-paced, emotionally-charged read Ms. Lennox has delivered in this book.... The way this story started had me hooked immediately."

—*Harlequin Junkie* on *The Baby They Longed For*

CHAPTER ONE

'MY BROTHER'S AN autocratic, over-indulged idiot. Yes, he's a skilled surgeon, but his people skills leave a lot to be desired. Now he's injured, from a stupid act of bravado caused by his failure to wait for the proper emergency services. He's accepted the care of his niece—*our niece*—but in his condition he's the last person fit for the task.'

That statement had been made two days ago. The woman had arrived at Dr Kiara Brail's veterinary-clinic-cum-animal-refuge unannounced. She'd introduced herself as Lady Beatrice Stonehouse, striding imperiously in without an appointment, almost a caricature of English aristocracy: a stocky, strident woman, ridiculously dressed for the Australian springtime in a tweed suit and stout shoes. Her clipped British accent had obviously been accustomed to delivering decrees, not asking for advice.

'I need to return to England,' she'd announced. 'I only came over to take care of the child until my brother was released from hospital. I won't trust my husband with my horses and dogs any longer, but I can't leave this pair without something to hold onto. In my opinion, a dog or a horse are the only solutions—aren't they the answer to everything? With that stupid designer house my brother insists on living in, horses are out of the question, so it needs to be a dog. I've done my research. Your establishment has the best reputation for matching dogs with difficult owners, and my brother's certainly difficult. Both of them are. I can't get a word out of the child. But if you can find the right dog for them and get it settled, I'm prepared to be more than generous.'

And she'd named a figure that had taken Kiara's breath away. And made her think.

Kiara had far too many clients for the dogs she had available. She didn't need to find another home for one of her dogs, but the builder's advice she'd received the day before had been terrifying. Termites. Foundations no longer fit for purpose.

Money she didn't have.

Which explained why Kiara was now standing outside the gates of what looked to be almost a mansion. She was in Clovelly, one of the most beautiful coastal suburbs of Sydney. It was also one of the most expensive. The gates she was standing in front of managed to be both discreet and imposing. No massive lions guarded this entrance, there was just exquisite ironwork set back from the boundary, with a gorgeous garden in front. The owner was obviously prepared to sacrifice a few metres of land to give the public a gorgeous vista to walk past, and make his entrance more…

Daunting was the word that came to mind.

She could see glimpses of the house through the wrought iron. The house was set low, built of pale stone, seemingly almost part of the cliffs. She could see a wide parking area, paved with the same soft stone. Enough parking for half a dozen cars? She bet there was garaging as well. She could see the glimmer of a swimming pool behind the trees. And the garden…

She thought of her own tangle of garden back at Birralong in the Blue Mountains. That was a glorious muddle, a mixture of English cottage planted by her grandmother, mixed with the ever-encroaching bushland.

She wouldn't part from her rambling, dilapidated home and her beloved Two Tails animal refuge for the world, but for a moment she indulged in just a tad of envy. What could she do if she had a tenth of the money this house was worth?

Get rid of termites?

And that was why she was here, she told herself sharply. All she had to do was to find a home for one of her needy dogs, and to part Bryn Dalton—whoever he was—with some of his hard earned.

Or hard inherited. Lady Stonehouse had been blunt. 'My half-brother is very wealthy. We all are. Our parents were unsatisfactory to say the least, but they've left us all…' She'd corrected herself then. 'They've left us *both* well provided for.'

Well, I'm not here to be intimidated by wealth, Kiara told herself firmly, and took a deep breath and pressed the central button on the very intimidating intercom.

And waited.

The silence seemed to go on for ever. Kiara had taken the train from her home in the Blue Mountains—much more sensible than trying to drive in city traffic—and had walked along the cliff path to this house. The street was silent, apart from the squawk of lorikeets in the flowering gums, and the wattle birds in the frangipani trees forming an avenue for the wealthy homes.

'He'll be home,' Lady Stonehouse had told her. 'He's injured his leg—badly. A crushed knee—he needed a complete replacement. He's now doing rehab at home. He'd like me to stay longer to help with the child, but I can't help any more than I have. If he thinks I'm hanging over his shoulder he's even less likely to agree to this proposal. Stupid man.'

If I had Lady Stonehouse hanging over my shoulder I might be tempted to disagree, too, Kiara thought. It sounded as if this man was being coerced to see her. This visit might well be a waste of time.

She had to try. She pushed the intercom again, and almost jumped when a gruff voice finally answered.

'Are you the vet?'

'I'm Dr Kiara Brail,' she confirmed. 'Yes.'

There was another silence. Kiara glanced up and then quickly glanced down again. An overhead camera was angled so that, inside, Dr Bryn Dalton would be gazing straight at her.

He'd see a woman in her early thirties, dressed sensibly. Her clothes weren't as ridiculously sensible as Lady Stonehouse's tweeds, but she was wearing her best jeans and a soft white blouse. Her dusky skin, the shade she'd inherited from her indigenous grandmother, didn't take easily to make-up, so she wore little. She was short, thin and if she didn't tie back her mass of deep black curls they ran riot. Her father had described her to his friends as scrappy. *'She's built for work rather than decoration,'* he'd said, *'and at least she knows how to keep out of the way.'*

Right now she wanted to be six feet tall and

imposing. For some reason she felt very, very small.

And she also felt like telling this family to stick their offer. She was way out of her comfort zone.

She stared at her toes as she avoided giving whoever was behind that camera the satisfaction of seeing her face, and she reminded herself of why she was here. She had a refuge full of dogs who needed care. She had buildings that needed maintenance.

She was desperate for money.

Needs must when the devil drives. Why had that saying popped into her head right now? Was it the sensation of being overwatched by someone even his sister had described as being an autocratic, over-indulged idiot?

He can't be a complete idiot, she told herself. She'd checked him out on the Internet before she came—well, why wouldn't she? Apparently Bryn Dalton was a neurosurgeon. The articles she'd read had declared him to be top of his field, the go-to surgeon for the type of tricky brain surgery others wouldn't risk. His résumé was impressive, to say the least. So he wasn't an idiot—at least, not an idiot career-wise. In her thirty-two years Kiara had discovered there were many ways of being an idiot.

Like her being here, being checked out, while

the man doing the checking took his own sweet time figuring whether he'd admit her or not.

Enough. 'I'm billing your sister for this call,' she said, brusquely. 'I've been standing here for almost ten minutes and I work on billable hours. Billable minutes rounded up. You want to waste more of your sister's money by not letting me in?'

There was another pause. Oh, for heaven's sake. She turned on her heel and took two steps away.

The gate clicked open behind her.

She stopped. Took a deep breath. She was pretty angry now. No, make that very angry. These people in their huge houses, their privileged positions… They thought they held all the power.

'I'm sorry,' the voice said, and his voice did hold a note of apology. 'Please come in.'

Deep breath. Calm down, she told herself. She did have a temper, but she was good at supressing it, and now certainly wasn't the time to let it out.

There was serious money in this establishment. If she had to grovel a little to get some of it for her dogs, then so be it.

But she did vent a little by stomping up the beautifully paved driveway, then along the landscaped artistry of the perfect garden path to finally arrive at the front door.

She almost expected to have to knock again, but it opened seamlessly in front of her. No one was behind it. She stepped through and stood, solitary, in a version of interior decorator heaven.

The entrance hall was the size of her kitchen. She saw gleaming marble floors, vaulted ceilings, exquisite designer furniture—a hall table that had to be antique and French, and two perfectly useless chairs that no one would be stupid enough to sit on. There was a flower arrangement that if, as she guessed, it had been delivered by one of Sydney's top florists, must be worth more than a week's feed for her dogs.

Which was why she was here, she reminded herself, trying desperately not to be intimidated. Dog food.

But wow, she felt small. Like Oliver in *Charles Dickens*...cap in hand, please, sir, can I have—?

'Don't just stand there, come through.' The voice barked through the intercom above the door, and she almost jumped. Okay, she did jump. If ever there was a set-up designed to put the peasants in their place...

Deep breath. The door to the left of the hall was the only one open. The others were firmly closed.

Another deep breath and she walked through.

A study. Really? She thought of her own cubbyhole of a study and almost snorted. A library, then? A vast room lined with impressive books. Leather furniture. An enormous mahogany desk set into a bay window at the end of the room.

A man in a wheelchair, spinning from his desk to face her.

Her first impression was dark, both the room and its occupant. The room was all books, dark polished floor, deep brown leather, a mahogany desk. The window he'd been sitting at was surrounded by ferns outside, which made the room look designer perfect, but it didn't light the room more than absolutely necessary. He'd obviously been using a desk lamp, but it didn't show his face.

So all she could see was a dark figure, lean, bearded? Maybe just unshaved. His leg was on some sort of support in front of the wheelchair.

He wheeled from the desk to face her but made no move to come closer. Nor did she make any move to come further into the room. There was a moment's silence while he seemed to assess her, his shadowed eyes raking her from the toes up.

Oh, for heaven's sake…

'I'm Kiara Brail, and I'm pleased to meet you, Dr Dalton,' she said, trying very hard to sound brisk and professional. 'Your sister tells me you'd like a dog.'

'She's my half-sister and I personally want no such thing,' he snapped. 'This is Beatrice's half-cocked idea. A dog…' He took a deep breath, as if summoning patience. 'However… I agree, the child needs something, and I'm prepared to try. But I want nothing to do with the thing. As soon as I can get back to work, I'll barely be home. Beatrice has told me she's paying. It'll make her feel better and she can finally leave us, which is what we all want. So bring the dog, but the deal is that you stay here for a week to make sure the thing's settled, house-trained, not likely to disrupt my routine. If at the end of the week my niece wants it to stay and it's no fuss, then it's sorted. Otherwise, the dog goes, but you'll be paid regardless.'

Whoa.

In the middle of that extraordinary statement two words stood out.

'The thing.'

Two Tails wasn't a standard refuge. It was geared for finding the perfect companion for people whose need was great.

If a family wanted a perky puppy, if a tradesman wanted a boisterous mate, if someone wanted a dog for companionship and fun, then there were a myriad breeders and rescue organisations that provided any number of dogs. Two Tails, however, was a specific refuge for specific needs. Its role was to find the right dogs for the right people, with Kiara taking all the trouble in the world to make that match work.

Two Tails' specialty was taking in elderly animals where the owner was no longer able to care for them, often pets that would face euthanasia at most refuges, because how many people wanted to adopt an elderly pet with a very limited life span? And how many refuges were prepared to rehouse animals with elderly or disabled owners?

Two Tails was named for two reasons—one, for the saying 'happy as a dog with two tails', because that was Kiara's aim for all her charges, and two, because there was the truth that Kiara's dogs were mostly facing two tales: a before and after.

The local vets knew Kiara and knew her work. If someone's pet died and they thought they were too old or too worried about the future to get another, vets would often refer them to Two Tails. Conversely, if someone came tearfully in and said they were moving into a retirement village and couldn't take their beloved dog, and maybe it should be put down, Kiara would be called to assess the dog. If it fitted the criteria, she'd take it in and work with it, including retraining if necessary. No matter that it be a greying, aged retriever with maybe only a limited time left, if it was the right dog, she'd find it a new home.

It was a niche service. A great service. It worked because Kiara personally vetted each animal and each potential owner.

'So you don't want a dog,' she said now, trying to keep her instinctive revulsion to herself.

'I have enough on my plate.' There was a moment's silence, and she sensed he was trying to suppress anger. 'As you see, I've been injured. I need to concentrate on rehab, plus I'm up to my neck with work that's been put aside because of my injury. However, I've agreed to take on the care of my niece, and my sister says she needs a dog. Thus—'

'Why are you caring for your niece?'

That brought another silence. By this time she was expecting to be told to mind her own business, but instead he stared at her some more and then told it like it was.

'I have… I *had* two sisters,' he said, and suddenly he sounded weary. 'Half-sisters. We have three different mothers. Our father was indifferent to all of us, so we've had practically nothing to do with each other. Beatrice's the oldest—she lives in the UK. I'm the youngest and, as you can see, my home is here. Skye…well, until three months ago Skye lived in California where she, probably encouraged by her mother, seems to have made some very bad life choices. One of them was having a daughter. Alice is ten years old and until three months ago I'd never met her. Then out of the blue, Skye arrived here, insisting she and her daughter needed to stay. I let her—I'm barely home and there seemed no harm. I should have...'

He caught himself then, his face twisting as if in pain, and then forced himself to continue. 'No matter. There was nothing anyone could do. It seems Skye had come here with a plan. Dump Alice and...' He shook his head as if trying to shake off a nightmare. 'We don't need to go there, but two weeks after she arrived, Skye took her own life.'

And there was a stomach lurch.

Two minutes ago, Kiara's instinct had been to get out of this house, fast. Now...

Ten years old. A child brought to stay with a half-uncle she didn't know and was 'barely home'.

Her mother's death.

'I can't leave this pair without something to hold onto.'

Lady Beatrice's words echoed hollowly in her head. She stared at the man before her, and he stared back. As if he'd thrown her a challenge.

'Your leg?' she said, and it was a question. Once more she half expected to be told to butt out, but his face seemed to close even more. Her eyes were starting to adjust to the dim light now.

She'd thought he was bearded but he wasn't, just shadowed from maybe two or three days without shaving. With his dark hair, ruffled and unruly, and his deep-set eyes, he looked…

Haunted? It was a crazy adjective, but it was the one that came to mind.

And when he spoke again, his voice was clipped, distant, and she decided haunted was maybe appropriate. For she heard pain.

'My sister chose to throw herself off the cliffs down from the house. You've seen the cliffs around here? They don't leave any room for doubt. Unfortunately, she left a note, and Alice found it too soon. She followed her mother, saw her fall and tried to climb down. By the time I reached them Skye was gone but Alice was trapped far down, just below the high-tide mark. I rang emergency services but climbed down after her—there seemed no choice. Stupid—I fell as well, smashing my leg. But at least I ended up on the same ledge as Alice. The rescue chopper took us off an hour later.'

'Oh, no.'

'As you say,' he said, and he had his formal voice working again. 'So now there's no one for her. Beatrice says the child should go to boarding school, but she's silent and withdrawn and she's terrified of the prospect. So I'm letting her be until school starts again next term. But now Beatrice is demanding that she have a dog.'

To say her heart was twisted was an understatement. A ten-year-old kid…

But one thing Kiara had grown accustomed to in the world she lived in was her heart being twisted. People coming to her, asking for her to care for a beloved pet, tears streaming down their faces as they left. People coming to her in need—*I just need a pet to love…*

Pets of all sorts, neglected, abandoned, bereft. Somehow she had to sort them, make hard decisions. Which ones could she help?

And here was another ask. Could she help?

Here, however, there was a bottom line. 'But you don't want a dog?'

'All I want is my life back.' It was a savage snap. And then he seemed to catch himself, regroup. She could almost see him brace, finding the professional, businesslike side of himself.

'I'm a neurosurgeon,' he told her. 'A busy one. I practise surgery at Sydney Central. I'm also a professor at our local university, so I teach. I'm on any number of medical and hospital boards. I've had to put everything on hold because of this…'

'Because of Alice?' She couldn't help herself.

'The thing. Because of this...'

'Because of my leg,' he said, smoothly again

though, explaining professional needs. 'I smashed my kneecap and broke both tibia and fibula. Compound fractures. I've had to have a complete reconstruction. It'll be another month before I'm fit to stand for long periods, so I've accepted the role of carer until then. After that, Alice will have to go to boarding school.'

He must have seen the look on her face because his tone changed a little, became defensive.

'You know, I understand Alice. Oh, not the trauma, that's not something I've been burdened with, but she was brought up a loner and that's the way she likes it. Our family has money, so Skye was always able to pay for decent childcare. That's how Alice seems to have been raised—by paid staff. So she understands how to cope by herself. Of course, she's now being treated by psychologists—the best—I organised that. But she hardly saw Skye, so she can't have been all that attached. Give her a little more time to get over this trauma and I agree with Beatrice—she'll be better off at a good school.'

'And then?' Focus on what you're here for, Kiara told herself, trying hard to keep hold of her temper. Focus on her own area of expertise. Finding a home for her animals. 'What happens to the dog then?' she asked.

'It can stay here if it's no trouble,' he said, offhandedly. 'The staff will see to it, and I assume

Alice will come back here during school breaks. She has nowhere else. So if she wants the dog then she can keep it, but Beatrice tells me you're willing to take it back if we no longer need it.' He paused, looked at her face and seemed to see what she was thinking. Which was dismay. Almost hurriedly he added: 'However, I'll bow to your judgement. I've never kept an animal. If you think it's more satisfactory, I'm prepared to pay whatever you need to board it when it's not required. Maybe you could keep it for us, bringing it back every holiday.'

There was so much in that it almost took her breath away. She struggled with herself, fighting the urge to turn and walk straight out.

'So the dog is to be a tool for your niece's recovery?' She could scarcely make herself say it.

'Beatrice says your organisation is strapped for money, dependent on donations. I'd imagine you'd be grateful.'

'I'm not the least bit grateful. My dogs aren't things.'

And that caused a long silence.

Kiara was accustomed to the low light by now, and she could see him clearly. He must have been fit before his fall, she thought. He looked long and lean and muscled. He was wearing a faded T-shirt with a sports-type emblem discreetly on the chest—an expensive brand. His jeans had one leg cut off to accommodate a brace. He was looking straight at her—his hooded eyes direct and challenging—but all of a sudden she saw a wash of what looked like almost overpowering weariness.

For some reason she was hit by a vision of the many injured creatures she'd treated in her career as a veterinarian. Dogs and cats, hissing or snarling, but underneath just plain terrified.

But she wasn't here to treat an injured man and his orphaned niece—or even to care for such. She was here to find a home for one of her needy pets. She thought—with some regret—of the donation Beatrice had mentioned, but this was no home for a creature that had already undergone trauma.

'I'll let myself out,' she said, and he stared up at her in surprise.

'You won't help us?'

'I can't see that giving you a dog would help you at all,' she told him, gently now. She'd had a moment to pull herself together, and this was the voice she used when letting prospective clients down.

No, she couldn't let ninety-year-old Mavis have the active young Doberman she'd set her heart on. Could she maybe introduce Mavis to an elderly pug?

She'd been hit by a walking stick when she'd

suggested it, she remembered, and the memory almost made her smile. They'd compromised. Mavis had gone away with a whippet with a limp, and the pair had shared four happy years.

She couldn't see a solution here that was even remotely happy.

'I wish you all the best,' she said. 'But maybe...' This was way out of her area of expertise but she could sense pain underneath the brusqueness, and it wasn't just pain from an injured leg. All her professional life had been devoted to alleviating pain, emotional as well as physical, and she couldn't help herself. 'You say you've organised psychological help for your niece. I'm thinking... maybe it could help you as well?'

Another silence. A long one. Then those shadowed, hawk-like eyes met hers for the last time.

'Get out,' he said.

'I'm leaving,' she retorted, and did.

The kid needed a dog. That was what Beatrice had decreed.

What the kid really needed was parents. Parents who cared.

Left to the silence, Bryn returned to his desk. His work was waiting. He'd kept his teaching role. He had queries from a couple of students he needed to answer.

Instead he put his head on his hands and, just

for a moment, gave into despair. He'd almost yelled at the woman who'd just left. Bryn's mantra in life was control, and Dr Kiara Brail had shaken it. For a couple of horrible moments she'd made him feel as if his world was slipping away.

And right now, he felt as if it was.

A half-sister he hadn't even met had decided he'd be a suitable parent—no, make that guardian, he reminded himself—for her daughter. Even the word guardian was laughable. He knew nothing about parenting. He knew nothing about families.

Bryn's life was his work. Emotion, commitment, took time and effort, and it left you totally exposed. Hadn't he learned that almost before he could walk? His father had moved on to the next woman before he was out of nappies. His mother...well, the least said about his mother the better. He was raised by money, by staff. People who moved on.

He'd learned early that you never got close to anyone. His bachelor life suited him down to the ground. He put everything he knew into being the best neurosurgeon he could be—and he *was* a good one. He helped people with his work, but he didn't get close, but here he was, suddenly the only available family of a child he hadn't even known existed until this had happened. Beatrice wouldn't take her. There was no one else.

He'd accepted responsibility. He'd faced that in the weeks he'd had to spend in hospital, and by that time he'd already learned of the personal barriers the child had drawn up to protect herself. Beatrice might be right. A dog might help get her over these first hard months, but from his own experience he knew that to face boarding school, to face life, those barriers would need to be reinforced.

And there was no choice. They both had to move on. He had his work, his life. He'd support Alice as much as he could, but the bottom line was that she'd already learned to be alone.

He thought back to that gut-wrenching night when Skye had taken her own life. He remembered standing at the top of the cliff, looking down. Seeing his niece huddled on a ledge almost to the water line. Thinking for a moment that she looked dead.

Shining his flashlight and seeing her face turn up to him. Desperate.

He'd gone down. Or tried to go down. He'd rung the emergency services first—he'd had that much sense—and then he'd tried to do the impossible. How Alice had got down there he could never afterwards work out—she surely wouldn't tell him—but some massive internal emotion had set him inching down a crumbling cliff face to reach her.

He'd fallen—of course he'd fallen—and then there were two to be winched to safety, not one.

What use had he been? No earthly use at all. He should have used sense, not emotion. Surely Alice would have survived alone.

And there was life's most important lesson, instilled in each member of his dysfunctional family. Alone was the only way *to* survive.

It was okay, he told himself, trying to shake off the way the woman had made him feel. Things would sort themselves out. Alice would recover from the shock of her mother's death and go on to a life of independence. He'd support her as much as he could—with a good school, carers during the holidays, even a dog.

Or not a dog. What he'd heard from the woman who'd just left was scorn—*'My dogs aren't things'*—and also…pity?

He didn't need pity. His leg was healing. He'd get his life back.

But the pity hadn't been for his leg. Those last words… *'You've organised psychological help for your niece. Maybe it could help you as well?'*

Stupid. He almost had his life under control again. Who was this woman to suggest otherwise? She knew nothing about him and had no right to suggest such a thing.

His flash of anger had been stupid. He had things under control. All he needed was his leg fixed, his niece sorted...and to put out of his mind the flash of pity he'd seen in one impertinent vet's dark eyes.

She'd intended to stomp right out of there. What a waste. She'd come all the way into Sydney on a fool's errand. Not only had she wasted a morning, she'd also been caught emotionally, and she knew she wouldn't be able to forget this for weeks.

She felt guilty.

Which was nonsense, she told herself. There were psychologists looking after the child's needs. She had an aunt and an uncle. Kiara's job was looking out for the needs of the animals in her care, and just because her heart had been wrung...

By both of them, she thought tangentially. By the story of an orphaned child, but also by her uncle. Bryn Dalton might have come across as overbearing—autocratic, his sister had called him—but Kiara spent her career dealing with people relinquishing loved pets, or people desperate for something else to love. She knew emotional stress when she saw it.

But there was no way she could help. Her responsibility was to her refuge, to Two Tails and to the animals in her care. She had to haul herself together and get out of here.

She walked out of the front door—and there was a child, sitting cross-legged on the path leading to the gate. Blocking her way.

Kiara stopped and the child raised a pale, too-thin face to hers.

'My uncle says you're getting me a dog,' she said, and it was a flat, defiant challenge. 'I don't want one.'

The kid was small for ten, a bit too thin. Her fine blonde hair was wisping to her shoulders and she was dressed in shabby shorts and T-shirt. Kiara recognised the logo on her T-shirt as an absurdly expensive children's brand, but nothing else about her looked expensive. She looked a string bean of a kid. She had pale blue eyes, shadowed, and her hair was badly in need of a brush.

Was her face…tear-streaked?

Oh, heck. Kiara recognised a wounded creature when she saw one and leaving this kid and walking away was more than she could bear.

'You don't have to have one.' It was said automatically, an instinctive response to the situation that had been made clear to her.

This was nothing to do with her. She should just walk on past.

But Kiara would have had to step on the manicured garden to get past the child.

And besides...there was something in the way she was sitting.

Her statement hadn't been an aside, something to be tossed at her as she left. It was an invitation to discuss.

And somehow, Kiara sensed all the pain in the world behind that belligerent statement. *'I don't want one.'*

For some reason she was suddenly thinking of her own childhood, of her at about the same age this child was now. Of her father. Of a litter of pups from one of the farm dogs, watching buyers come and taking them away. Of her holding the smallest, pleading, *'Please can I keep him? Please can he be mine?'*

'Don't be stupid,' her father had barked. *'Dogs are for work. These are pedigree cattle dogs—we sell them for cash. Put the pup down.'*

Why was she thinking that now? Why was her heart lurching?

Don't get involved, she told herself harshly. Your responsibility is to your dogs.

But her heart was still twisting. Surely it wouldn't hurt to talk to the kid for a minute.

'You're Alice,' she said, and the child nodded. She was staring up at Kiara, almost as if challenging her. To do what?

'Why don't you want a dog?' she said and sat

down in the middle of the path with her. Cross-legged. Face to face.

The kid looked a bit taken aback. She edged back a little, but not far.

'I'm Kiara,' Kiara said, gently, lightly. 'Why don't you want a dog?' she said again.

'I'm not staying here. My mother says…said… I have to, but I don't.'

'You'll be going to school.'

'No.'

'So where else will you go?'

'I don't know.' And it was a wail of distress, a cry so deep and painful that Kiara flinched.

'You'll stay here.' It was a low growl and it made Kiara jump. Unnoticed, Bryn had silently wheeled along the path behind her. Maybe Alice had seen him come, maybe she hadn't, but she didn't react. She certainly didn't look at him.

'You'll stay here, for as long as you need to,' Bryn said, still gruffly. He was ignoring Kiara, concentrating solely on his niece. 'I've promised you that, Alice.'

'You don't want me. You never wanted me to come.'

'We're family. I'm your uncle.'

Wrong answer, Kiara thought tangentially. She thought, what would she have done given the same set of circumstances?

Who knew? She had no solid family herself, no well of life experience to draw on.

Except for the animals she loved—the bereft creatures that ended up in her charge.

She thought of one of the few cats she'd re-housed. Two Tails was geared to rehome dogs, but Mops had been an exception. She'd glimpsed him out in the bushland behind the refuge, trying to fend for himself. He was scrawny, his grey and white hair matted. He was also scarred, probably from encounters with the native possums.

Even if her emotions hadn't been caught, cats decimated the wildlife, so Kiara had set a trap for him. She'd caught him on the third night. He'd been wild, terrified, spitting his fury and his fear.

She'd fed him, talked to him, and gently, gently encouraged him to trust.

He was now living with an elderly man who'd lost his wife. The last time she'd seen him—on the home visit she made to all her rehoused animals—Mops had been sitting on his new owner's knee, purring so loudly it almost interfered with the television. Whenever the old man's hand stopped stroking, Mops shifted and nudged until the stroking continued. Both of them had been deeply content with the new arrangement.

And that's what this kid needs, she thought. Nights of holding, telling her she's loved.

Not an assurance such as *'You'll stay here,*

for as long as you need to.' That was an implied ending. Alice was expected to leave.

'I don't want the dog.' Alice jutted her jaw and met her uncle's look full on.

'You don't have to have a dog. Your aunt thought—'

'My aunt doesn't care.'

'She thought a dog might help. You might enjoy it. If Kiara—'

'It's Dr Brail,' Kiara said abruptly. She was here on a professional visit, she reminded herself, and it wouldn't hurt to remind them all of that. She might be sitting cross-legged on the path with a bereft child but, for her sake as well as anything else, she needed to keep this businesslike. 'I'm a doctor of veterinary science. I did my doctorate with a study of rehoming animals in need. But it seems I'm not needed here.'

'There's an open invitation,' Bryn said, still watching Alice. 'If you think it could help, then bring us a dog. Beatrice has offered to pay you to stay for a week and see what happens. You must see that Alice needs...something.'

'I want to go home,' Alice said.

'I'm sorry but you can't,' Bryn said, and once again, Kiara thought wrong answer. The answer should be *This is your home now.*

But she had things to do. Animals to care for. She'd been away from Two Tails for more than half a day and Maureen, the part-time assistant she could scarcely afford, would be aching to leave. Maureen was an old friend of her grandmother's, a woman who'd been there for her for ever, but she had her own family needs. She could ask no more of her.

This was a mess—an emotional nightmare—but it wasn't her nightmare. She rose, carefully closing her heart.

'Good luck to both of you,' she said softly. And then, even more softly, 'I'm so, so sorry that I can't help.'

And before her heart could be tugged a moment longer, she turned and fled.

The gate slid silently closed, leaving Bryn staring down at his little niece. Alice didn't move, just sat on the path with her arms crossed. As if shielding herself from pain?

He needed to contact the psychologists again. He knew she was hurting, but what could he do?

'I don't want a dog.' It was a muttered whisper, barely audible.

'You don't have to have one.'

'I want to go home.'

'You have an appointment with Dr Schembury tomorrow. You can talk about that then.'

Silence. Hell, he was so far out of his depth.

The words of the woman who'd just left was

still replaying in his head. *'Psychological help... maybe it could help you as well?'*

It wouldn't help at all. What good could talking do? For Alice, yes, but for him... He didn't open up about emotions. Why should he?

Alice rose and slipped away. Who knew where? To another part of the garden? Back to her own room where she could be solitary? Safe?

Solitude helped, he thought. It worked for him.

But for some reason he was left staring at the closed gate, seeing a slip of a woman with pity in her eyes.

He didn't need pity. His leg would heal. The psychs would sort Alice and she'd learn to be strong. He didn't need Dr Kiara Brail and her dogs.

But Alice?

She didn't want a dog either. She didn't want... him.

He thought of the night he'd found her, huddled on the cliff ledge, desperate. Of holding her, trying to keep her safe. Of her despairing whisper. *'I want Mom.'*

She didn't want him, but he was all she had.

He thought of the psychologists in their hospital consulting rooms, empathising, asking all the right questions, treating Alice by the book.

And he thought again of Kiara, sitting cross-legged on the path, acting almost like a kid herself. Who was she to succeed where the psychologists couldn't?

No one, he thought. And anyway, she'd refused to help.

Because she didn't like his terms?

Maybe...

'You're clutching at straws,' he told himself bleakly. 'She's knocked back Beatrice's offer and what would Beatrice know anyway?'

What would Dr Kiara Brail know?

'Nothing,' he said out loud and that was that.

But why, as he turned and wheeled back to the house, did the look in her eyes stay with him? A look that said she understood the pain Alice was feeling. A look that said, given half a chance, she might just be a friend to his damaged niece.

A friend to him?

'Ridiculous,' he said. He—and Alice—had enough to worry them without including a slip of a vet who also had judgement in that same gaze. She was judging him and finding him wanting?

So what?

'Forget her,' he told himself and wheeled inside and allowed the big front doors to close silently behind him. Closing out the thought of that judgement?

It didn't quite happen.

CHAPTER TWO

SHE DIDN'T HAVE the right pet anyway.

All the way home on the train, Kiara told herself over and over: 'They don't need a dog. They need help far above anything the addition of a dog can cure.'

They needed help far above anything *she* could cure.

She'd brought her laptop with her. She had plenty of work she should be getting on with as she travelled, but instead she found herself staring out of the window. But she wasn't looking at the scenery, which grew more and more breathtaking as she neared her Blue Mountains home. Instead she saw a wisp of a kid declaring she didn't want a dog. A kid who, in some intangible way, reminded her of the lonely child she'd once been.

Alice has it much, much worse than I ever did, she told herself, and that made her feel even more bleak.

As did the thought of… A man who looked gutted?

He's nothing to do with me, she told herself. He's rich, arrogant and insensitive. He doesn't want a dog. He just wants to get rid of responsibilities.

But when she got back to Two Tails she couldn't help herself. She leafed through the files of the dogs she had in care, and then went out to check the pens, greeting the dogs in question, asking herself…could this one help?

And of course there wasn't one.

Two Tails was a refuge with specific aims. It was Kiara's dream refuge, a vision she'd had since she was…well, as long as she could remember.

The animals on her father's farm had been just that, animals. A means to an income. Her father had never treated his livestock badly—that'd hurt his income. But he'd never looked at an animal with anything other than consideration of how useful it could be.

The same went for how he saw his daughter. Kiara's mother had walked out when she was six, and in fairness Kiara couldn't blame her. She'd married a cold, hard man. The only thing Kiara blamed her mother for was not taking her with her, and hearing of her mother's death a couple of years later had only cemented that feeling of abandonment.

So Kiara had been left with her father, who treated her as a nuisance when she was small and free labour as she grew. But she'd also been left with her father's animals. He never knew that she had a name for every one of them, that she cried her eyes out every market day.

So Two Tails was her answer. Early on she'd set her heart on being a vet, but the aim of veterinary science, for Kiara, was to give as many animals as possible as good a life as she could manage. She ran a normal clinic at the rear of Two Tails—she had to do something to earn a living and the tiny town of Birralong appreciated having a resident vet—but the rest of the time she spent matching relinquished pets with those who most needed them.

And that didn't include Bryn Dalton, she told herself as she walked from pen to pen. But still she found herself thinking…

The little Peke whose owner had died unexpectedly two weeks ago? The relatives had taken the dog to a vet on the other side of Sydney. 'Can you put it down, please? There's no one to look after it.'

Pamela the Peke was ten years old and spent her life trying to find a lap for a cuddle. She also yapped, but that was a small price to pay for a friend. Kiara had a score of clients waiting; she just had to decide the best match.

But a yappy Peke for Bryn? No, she corrected herself. She'd meant to think, a yappy Peke for Alice? Either way the answer was no.

Who else? The wolfhound in the next pen? Ralph was gorgeous but aging, and wolfhounds had such a limited life expectancy. The last thing Alice needed was another heartbreak, and she had two alternative clients wanting Ralph already.

A whippet? Maybe, but the whippet in question was a bit stand-offish. Kiara's career was matching people with pets, and she just knew they wouldn't suit.

It was the same for all the dogs in her charge, she decided, and then she thought that it was just as well because if there'd been such an animal she would have been torn.

And she couldn't have helped, even if she was torn.

'Kiara?' The voice came from the front yard, hauling her out of her thoughts of the two people she'd met that morning.

Hazel.

Hazel Davidson was pretty much Kiara's best friend. They'd met at university, had bonded over their love for animals, and Hazel had helped Kiara set up Two Tails.

Two Tails was established on the property that Kiara's grandmother had left her, but establishing the refuge had cost money neither of them had. They'd worked side by side at a vet clinic in Coogee until they'd saved enough to set the refuge up. But the refuge and tiny clinic didn't provide an income to support them both, so Kiara worked here full-time, and Hazel came when she could.

Kiara wasn't surprised at her arrival. What she was surprised at, though, was the urgency she heard in her friend's voice.

'Kiara, where are you?'

'In the pens. Hang on, I'm coming…' she called out and headed out to see what the matter was.

Kiara's grandma had been an indigenous Australian. She'd married an Irishman who'd died soon after the birth of their only child—Kiara's mother—and she'd lived at Birralong ever since. Her passion had been the native bushland and the garden within the house yard, and she'd eked a living by propagating and selling plants. When she'd died, the garden had been overgrown but gorgeous. It was gorgeous still. Kiara walked into the front yard now and saw Hazel stooped over something lying under the shade of a native frangipani. The soft yellow blooms were wafting down on Hazel's head and the perfume was everywhere.

But this was no time for taking in the beauty of the place. What was the urgency? She headed down the path—and stopped short.

A dog. A collie? Hard to say from here.

Hazel was bent over it. What…?

'I found her on the side of the road near the bus stop in Birralong,' Hazel told her. 'She's… Oh, Kiara, this is just awful…'

There was a stomach lurch. This had happened before. The bus stop was at the corner, right by the sign to her clinic. What was it about the sign 'Veterinary Clinic' that made people feel they had a licence to dump animals nearby? Kiara crouched by her friend, seeing what Hazel was seeing.

A border collie. Small for its breed. Black and white.

But this was no healthy dog suffering simply from road trauma. Kiara had seen neglected dogs in the past but this…

Hazel sat back, tears in her eyes, as Kiara moved in to check. The dog was lying on its side—*her* side—on the grass. Her bones stood out with horrific clarity. Kiara could see grazes along her side and her legs, from the bitumen on the road? What fur she had left was filthy and matted. But there was worse.

There were deep sores around her neck—a gouge where, at first guess, she thought a rope must have fastened so tight it had dug in. There were still traces of rope left in the wounds. Her hindquarters were a mass of pressure sores. She looked as if she'd spent her life sitting at the end of some appalling roped existence, with no choice but to sit, and sit, and sit. Or lie.

There were similar sores along her ribs, and her thigh… It was swollen, oozing. A massive infection?

Kiara put her hand gently on the dog's head. She expected nothing. The dog looked too far gone to flinch, to snarl, to react.

The little collie did none of these things, but instead of passive stillness, as Kiara's hand moved under her head to cradle and lift, the collie's eyes widened. Big, dark eyes met hers.

She saw calmness.

Trust?

And as she shifted her hand to see the damage, the dog raised one filthy, matted paw to rest on her arm. Like a plea for help?

If ever there was a heart twist, this was it. A dog, appallingly mistreated, looking up at her as if humans were to be trusted. As if Kiara was to be trusted.

'Can we even do anything to help her?' Hazel's voice was a wretched whisper. 'It might be kinder to… On top of everything else that's happened today, I don't think I can bear it.'

What was happening with Hazel? Kiara cast her a concerned glance, but her attention had to be solely on the dog. She could hardly tear her gaze from that of the dog. These wounds were indeed horrific but…

'She's only young,' she whispered. 'Maybe…'

'Oh, Kiara, look at her. She's been so abused that, even if we did manage to save her life, how scarred is she going to be? Physically and emotionally? Then there's the cost. Who's going to pay? We both know that sometimes the kindest thing to do is…is to let them go. We can make sure she's not in any pain.'

The dog's head was still in Kiara's hands, and she was still looking into those trusting dark eyes. But Hazel was right, she thought grimly. What lay ahead if she decided to treat were X-rays, blood tests, and who knew what else? Then coping with infections, refeeding programmes, months of treatment. And after this amount of mistreatment the dog might end up a snarling, terrified neurotic. Who could blame her?

But those eyes… That paw, still resting on her arm…

She took a deep breath. 'We're going to do more than that,' she said. 'Let's get her into the surgery. I know it doesn't make sense, and we can't afford to take on a case like this but, dammit, Hazel, we set up Two Tails for a reason. If I'm going to end up bankrupt, then I'll go down doing what I do to the end.'

They carried the dog into their clinic at the side of the house. They X-rayed and, thanks be, found no breaks. No sign of major internal blood loss from injuries like a ruptured spleen or liver.

They set up an IV to rehydrate. They organised anaesthetic—no easy feat in a dog so near death—and then they worked together to painstakingly get rid of the matted fur so they could clean and debride the myriad foul sores.

The thigh was the major problem. The wound had ulcerated and the infection was deep. And the smell…

Clostridial myositis? That was a heart sink, but the look of the wound, the smell… Years ago she'd seen a similar wound in a horse that had been left unchecked for too long. The owner had elected to have the animal put down.

Sensible? Yes, it was, but now…those eyes… that paw…

'I'm suspecting clostridium myositis,' she said grimly, and Hazel looked at her in astonishment. She'd settled now, emotion taking a back seat to allow veterinary competence to hold sway. They were two vets, two friends, working their hardest to save a dog that would cost Kiara a mint.

'How can you tell?'

'I'll need blood tests to be sure, but I've seen it before.'

'Oh, Kiara…'

And she knew what Hazel was thinking. Kiara's focus was on her role, coping with the ulceration of the thigh, but some part of her was still conscious of Hazel's reminder of money—or the lack of it. The astronomical quote to repair termite damage had been hanging over her since she'd first seen it, growing more and more impossible, and in the silence as they worked it seemed to grow even bigger.

'We can fix this.'

'Yeah, but the cost.'

'Let's just do it.'

What followed were hours of meticulous work, to clean and debride what seemed an endless number of lesions. And because Hazel was her friend, because they were used to working together and knew exactly what they were doing, they were able to distract themselves a little by talking about other things. Even if they were also unpleasant.

'Have you any idea how you might cover costs?' Hazel asked as they worked.

'Why bother?' She shook her head, the dreariness of her situation closing in. 'What's another debt among so many? Two Tails is doomed to close anyway.'

'What?' Hazel had known they were strapped for cash, but not about this latest disaster. 'No!'

'I got a quote to repair the termite damage and it's...well, it's impossible. Even if I mortgaged the property to find the money, I wouldn't be able to meet the repayments.'

'You can't close!' It was an exclamation of horror. 'What if you charged more?'

'How? By taking in more dogs and selling them to the highest bidder? That's not how we do things.'

'Publicity, then?' Hazel asked slowly.

She thought about it. Hazel's boss, Finn, was a celebrity vet, hosting a TV show called *Call the Vet*. Finn would know all about publicity—but her shy friend? Not so much.

'I took part in an episode of *Call the Vet* that was being filmed today and I talked about Two Tails,' Hazel told her, sounding a bit self-conscious. 'The show's producer is interested in coming out here and doing an episode, and with a bit of luck it could lead to donations.'

'Wait a minute.' Kiara's interest was caught. 'I thought you swore over your dead body that you'd never appear in that programme again.'

'I did. But there was a hit and run outside the clinic.' Hazel shrugged. 'I guess it comes with the territory but this one got to me. A gorgeous old black spaniel who's apparently a stray. He needed surgery to plate a tibial fracture. Finn thought he must be about fourteen or fifteen years old. He also needed a name, so I called him Ben.'

So that was what had made it so awful. Two abandoned dogs in one day.

But… Ben?

'Ben? Wasn't that your first ever dog?'

'Yeah.'

'So we're both suckers for dogs.'

'I guess we are.'

They worked on for a bit, but there was something about Hazel. Something she wasn't saying.

'Well, then,' Kiara prodded. 'Was that what made it a bad day for you? Having to work with Finn? Or did Ben not make it?'

'Ben's doing well, as far as I know,' she said diffidently. 'I'll go and check on him when I'm done here.' There was a self-conscious pause and then, 'It's Finn who's not doing so well. A baby got left in the waiting room with a note that said it was his.'

'No! Tell me!'

So she did. It seemed as if Hazel's boss had

been landed with a baby. A baby he swore he didn't know.

As they carried on chatting about Finn's predicament more and more of the dog's matted hair fell away. She could now see clearly what she was dealing with, and as the dog's breathing stayed steady, Kiara was starting to feel positive again. There was nothing like a bit of gossip to make a girl forget her troubles.

So...why not share?

'I had my own share of drama today, too,' she told Hazel, and as she worked she told her about Beatrice's visit, and her own trip to meet Bryn and his little niece.

'The amount she offered me was ridiculous,' she told her. 'And I don't even have a dog suitable for a child.'

'How about this one?' Hazel asked, and Kiara stopped what she was doing and stared. Then she stared down at the ragged, skeletal dog they were working on.

'Are you out of your mind?'

'Maybe.' Hazel paused as well and stood back, looking at the dog they were treating. Surely no one would want this dog, at least not for months, and even then, not if her temperament proved impossible. 'But it sounds as if there are two wounded souls that need help. Why not make it three?'

'Hazel, that's ridiculous.'

'You'll need to find a home for her, even if you are bankrupt,' she said, reasonably. 'Especially if you're bankrupt. You know, I've sort of fallen for her, too. Why not give her to someone who can pay?'

And for a crazy moment Kiara let herself think it might be possible. She let her thoughts drift forward…

'Maybe I could call her Bunji,' she murmured, thinking back to her grandmother, who often slipped into her First Nation language. 'It means a mate. A friend.' She smiled ruefully then, hauling herself back to reality. 'Who am I kidding? How could I give such a dog to a ten-year-old?'

'Give her to the uncle. He sounds like he needs a friend, as much if not more than his niece. And hey, if he falls for Bunji he might even be prepared to backpay for her treatment. How's that for a thought?'

Okay. For a moment Kiara let herself seriously consider.

She thought of the pair of them, of their underlying desperation.

She thought of Bryn.

For some reason Hazel's words resonated. *'He sounds like he needs a friend, as much if not more than his niece.'* She thought of his shadowed face. Of the pain she saw, a pain that wasn't just physical.

That's not my problem, she told herself fiercely. She had enough problems of her own to deal with.

'They really don't want a dog.' She tried to say it with authority, tried to believe it was true. 'Besides, I'd have to stay there. A week at least, he stipulated, and who's going to take care of this place? I can't ask you to take more time off.' Hazel had used her last holidays helping her build new pens, and there had to be limits to how much she could ask. 'I can't afford to pay anyone. The whole thing's impossible.'

She looked down again at… Bunji. How had that name stuck so fast? She looked like something out of an anatomical diagram, Kiara thought grimly. Almost skeletal.

And yet part of Kiara was still caught by the look in the dog's eyes as she'd carried her inside, as she'd organised the anaesthetic. There'd been such trust…

And then Hazel's phone beeped and beeped again. Whoever was trying wanted her urgently.

They'd done almost as much as they could do tonight. Hazel cast her an apologetic glance, stripped off her gloves and went to check. She read and her face changed.

'I need to go,' she said.

'Ben?'

'I…no. I'm sure he's okay but I would like to see for myself. And you'll want the results on those blood samples as soon as possible.'

Kiara nodded. 'No worries. We've done all we can for the moment. I'll finish up and get her settled. Thanks so much for your help.'

'Think about what I said before,' Hazel said as she gathered her gear. 'About giving Bunji to that uncle. Maybe it's true that people—and dogs—come into our lives for a reason.'

'Maybe,' she said, as the door closed behind Hazel. Then she sighed. 'Or maybe not. Oh, Bunji. Mate. What are we going to do?'

CHAPTER THREE

WHAT FOLLOWED WAS a dire couple of weeks, taking care of her dogs, trying to salvage the wreck that was Bunji, trying to figure a way she could keep Two Tails running—and finally there was a frank discussion with her bank manager. Who put it to her straight.

'Your best bet is to put the place on the market right now,' he'd told her. 'It'll never sell as an animal refuge. We suggest you pull the pens down and present it as a possible luxury home. A renovator's delight if you will, and there are plenty of cashed-up couples who'll buy it as such. What you get should leave you a little to go on with—enough to rent a place in town and give you enough time to search for work.'

The thought broke her heart, but she was starting to accept it. She was already starting to wind down, figuring how long it would take to rehome the pets she had, how long it would take to walk away.

But not from Bunji.

The little collie was doing brilliantly, though only a vet might say so. To an untrained observer she still looked like a train wreck. The diagnosis of clostridial myositis had been confirmed, and the wound on her thigh was finally starting to heal. Her fur was starting to grow back but she still looked half shaved.

She slept now in a crate by Kiara's bed. Not because she needed the warmth of the house—the spring weather was warm enough for her to be safe in one of the pens—but because those eyes followed Kiara, almost as an act of desperation. She never whined; she never made any demands. She just looked as though being close was all she asked in life.

It would take months before she could be made presentable enough—trusting enough—to rehouse with Kiara's usual needy clients. So wherever she went, Bunji would have to come with her, Kiara thought, but the impossibility of finding a rental that'd take her—and the unfairness of leaving such a dog while she was forced to take a full-time job…

The future was filling all her thoughts and she almost missed the blinking on her phone that told her she'd missed a call. It was from Hazel; she'd left a voicemail.

'I'm heading your way. I'll fill you in when I

get there, but it's best if I get away from here and I need to go somewhere I can take Ben. I don't know if that job opportunity's still there—the one with that guy who needs you to live in and get a rehome settled?—but if it is this might be the ideal time to take advantage of it. I'm more than happy to take care of Two Tails for a week or so.'

She rang her back. Her friend was already driving. She pulled over to take the call, and sounded abrupt. 'Could you still take that job at…what was the guy's name? The guy with the niece who wanted Bunji?'

'He didn't want Bunji.'

'But he needed Bunji. And he'll pay. Kiara, I have… I have a week or so off. I can care for Two Tails if you still want to go.'

What the…? 'Have you been sacked?'

There was a loaded silence. 'No,' Hazel said at last. 'But…it's complicated. If this guy is still offering that sort of money…'

'It was his sister who was offering.'

'But it's huge, right? Maybe enough to keep Two Tails going for a while longer?'

'He doesn't want a dog.' How many times had she said that, mostly in her own head, over the last two weeks?

'So take the week to find out. What's the alternative?'

'Hazel…'

'Just do it,' Hazel told her.

So she did.

CHAPTER FOUR

THE VET WAS HERE. Bryn had agreed, and now he was regretting it.

What Alice surely needed was someone skilled in treating neglected, traumatised kids, but by now Alice had been under the care of the best children's psychologists he could find. Bryn's medical network was wide. The people he'd found were skilled, but they'd made no difference at all.

Alice was aloof to the point of clinical detachment. She was outwardly a biddable, obedient child. She slept, woke, dressed, ate—though not enough. She answered politely when questioned. When the psychologists worked with her, Bryn got the impression she was expecting every question, had heard it all before.

What sort of life had she led until now? After a lot of research, he'd managed to locate the last of the many temporary nannies and housekeepers Skye had employed back in the States. The woman had been blunt.

'I only worked with them for a month, and that was all I could stand. I was sorry for Alice but there was no way I could help. The mother threw money around like water, but she was screwed up. To her the kid was just a nuisance—or a servant when everyone else quit, which was often. She used to scream at us to get out of the house and I can't tell you the hours I spent at the park, with Alice staring into middle distance, engaging in nothing at all. I couldn't get through to her. So her mom's died? I'm sorry to hear it, but part of me thinks it's the only hope the kid has. Good luck with her.'

So he'd spent the weeks while his own leg healed, waiting for Alice to heal. But her mental wounds seemed so much worse than his physical injuries. She sat in her bedroom or out in the garden and she stared at nothing. Waited for… nothing?

And now, weeks after that initial approach, the vet with the dog had finally agreed to take up his sister's offer. She'd agreed to bring a suitable dog here, she'd stay for a week or so, and she'd see if it could make a difference. Nothing else was working and Beatrice was on his case, so why not accept?

He'd researched Two Tails by now, a do-good

organisation run on a shoestring. A little digging had him discovering its founder, Dr Kiara Brail, was in dire financial difficulties. For all the contempt she'd shown him at their first meeting, he knew she'd have accepted this job for money. She'd offload one of her dogs, she'd get some much-needed cash and be out of here. She'd said she had a dog she thought might be suitable, but he'd cut her off. He wanted no details. He was pretty much certain Alice would take one look at any fluffy bit of yappery and…

No. She wouldn't even look, he thought. Every single thing he'd produced for her, every suggestion, every attempt to get close, had been met with a blank stare, a polite response and then indifference.

But he couldn't get away from the fact that Alice was deeply unhappy. Her remoteness was a shell he couldn't pierce, but for a ten-year-old to have no joy at all… The longer it lasted, the more desperate he felt.

The return call from Dr Brail had come at a time when he was feeling at his wits' end. The sensations he'd felt when he'd first met her were still with him. He didn't need her pity—or her judgement—but for Alice… Okay, he'd try anything he could, even if it did mean infringing even more on his precious isolation.

So he'd agreed to her coming, but when the

doorbell went he made his way out to greet her thinking this would be another week wasted. Luckily this house was big enough to keep them all separate.

He opened the door and here she was, the woman he remembered. Little, dark, fiery.

Fiery? That had been the adjective that had come to mind when he remembered her. He'd been pretty much out of it when he'd interviewed her last, seeing her as someone his sister had foisted onto him. Businesslike, determined, she'd hardly dented his radar—until she'd fired up. *'My dogs aren't things.'* He'd got it, he'd even admired her for it.

It didn't help his opinion of her now, though, when he knew she'd accepted Beatrice's offer because she needed cash.

But she was here, and he might as well make the most of it. She stood on his doorstep wearing jeans and a plain shirt—pretty much the same as he'd seen her the last time.

Her dark curls were tugged back tight.

She was wearing a battered backpack, and at her side was probably the most appalling dog he'd ever seen.

It was a black and white border collie—or at least what fur it had was black and white. It looked a mass of healing sores. Its thigh was shaved and dressed with a thick white wad. One of its ears looked torn—its good ear pricked up as if interested, the other flopped uselessly down, as if a muscle had been torn. Its eyes were too big for a face that looked almost cadaverous. It was wearing a harness and lead, but it stood pressed against her leg, as if it needed her support.

It looked…appalling.

'What the hell is this?'

He spoke instinctively and he spoke too loud. Both the dog and the woman flinched. But Kiara didn't back away. She stooped and lifted the dog into her arms and held her close.

'This is Bunji,' she told him, defiance front and centre as she met his gaze head-on. 'Bunji's had almost as hard a time in life as Alice. I thought they might help each other.'

'I don't need another…'

'Another what?' Her chin tilted. Her eyes held anger, pure and simple.

Another what? Another hopeless creature? Her words held condemnation and he deserved it. But he was floundering.

'You can't foist another…'

'I'm not foisting anything on anyone. You want me to leave, I will.'

He stared at them both, woman and dog. Her eyes didn't leave his. She was cradling the dog—surely too big for her to carry—against her breast, and the dog was huddling against her.

While he watched, it suddenly raised its head and licked her, throat to jaw. A measure of trust.

And suddenly he felt ashamed. He'd read of the work this woman did. Two Tails Animal Refuge… Yes, she was here because she needed money, but she needed money because of the work she did.

But this dog?

'My niece doesn't need this dog,' he said, sure of his ground on this one. 'She's wounded herself. For heaven's sake, we need something to cheer her up.'

'What's foist?'

The voice came from behind him. Alice had simply appeared, a silent wraith, watching on the sidelines of life. Even getting two words from Alice was unusual.

He turned. The little girl, dressed as always in the shabby shorts and shirt she seemed to live in—she loathed it when his housekeeper insisted they had to be washed—was hard at his heels, staring out at the dog in Kiara's arms.

What had he said? *'You can't foist another...'*

'A gift,' Kiara said promptly. 'Foist means give a gift. Your uncle was saying I can't give another gift to him. I guess that meant you were the first gift. Bunji is the second. If you both want her, that is.' And she set the dog gently down again by her side.

There was a deathly silence while Alice stared at Bunji, and Bryn felt a surge of gratitude so great it threatened to overwhelm him. This kid had been through so much. The last thing she needed was to think her uncle didn't want her.

The fact that he didn't…

No. It was no longer true, he accepted. When he'd woken in hospital to realise what Skye had done, he'd felt overwhelmed. Injured, battered, shocked, all he'd wanted in that moment was to get his old life back. But in these past weeks, as his pain levels had decreased, as he'd done the research on his niece's background, as he'd had the space in his head to see Alice's needs, he'd come to realise that even if he could wish Alice away, he wouldn't. If some magical relative appeared from the States ready to transport his niece back overseas to a happy ever after, he'd at least follow. He'd at least make sure the kid was safe.

He'd want to stay involved.

But try as he might to find one, there was no such relative, and now, as he watched Alice watch the dog, as he thought of Kiara's words—*a gift*—he thought just maybe…

'It's hurt?' Alice said it tentatively, but the words themselves were important. She spoke so rarely. *Please…thank you…yes…no.*

Mostly no.

'This is Bunji and she's very hurt,' Kiara said, gently now, speaking only to Alice. 'She's just one year old—she's little more than a baby—but she's had a very bad time. The people who had her didn't look after her. They bought her as a cute puppy and then they seemed to forget about her. They hardly fed her, they never let her play and when they decided they didn't want her any more they threw her away. She's been lonely and hungry and afraid all her life. My friend Hazel found her on the side of the road, all by herself. She brought her to me because I care for dogs like Bunji. I've treated her sores, I've fed her and cared for her, but what she needs now, most in the world, is someone who wants to be a friend. Someone who cares for her. Bunji's an Australian word for friend, and for some reason I thought that friend might be you. If you think you might be able to help. And if your uncle agrees, of course.'

'She looks far too damaged to be out of care.' Bryn's words were too harsh. He caught himself, backtracked, tried to soften. 'I mean… Dr Brail, surely this dog needs more treatment than we can give? Even if Alice wanted her…'

'That's why I need to come and stay for a while,' Kiara said calmly, still looking at Alice. 'To teach you both how to care. Alice, do you remember me? I came here a couple of weeks ago.

My name's Kiara. Your aunty Beatrice asked me to stay with you for a week, for you to get to know Bunji. To see if you'd like Bunji as a friend.'

The little girl was still staring at the dog. 'Would she only be here for a week?' It was a flat response, but at least it was a response. In answer Kiara fondled the dog's ears and looked at Bryn. Her gaze said the next answer was up to him. The response was something she had no business giving. This was between him and his niece.

He stared down at the dog. A more miserable, wounded, neglected creature he'd never seen.

Alice was looking at the dog as well. Saying nothing. Standing back. Waiting.

Would she only be here for a week?

He looked at Kiara, who looked blandly back at him. This was his call. Dammit, why couldn't she have brought something cute? Something a kid could really love?

Love? He thought suddenly, tangentially, of the women he'd dated before Skye's suicide had propelled him so viciously into uncharted waters. He'd been a serial dater. With his money, his looks, his professional connections, the world had pretty much been his oyster. He'd dated some gorgeous women in his time.

But...*love*? Why was the word suddenly wobbling, as if it had some kind of meaning he hadn't figured?

And maybe Alice got it before he did. She took a couple of tentative steps forward. Kiara was cradling the dog's head, holding it steady. Was she holding the dog's head to prevent snapping? If it was vicious…

'She's a bit scared,' Kiara said gently to Alice. 'She hasn't met many people who are kind to her.'

'People hurt her?' It was a whisper.

'They did. They didn't love her, and they threw her away when they didn't want her any more.'

She didn't say more, and he had the sense to stay silent himself. They stood in the early morning sunshine, while girl and dog seemed to take stock of each other.

Most young dogs would have sniffed forward, Bryn thought. Investigated. Or pulled back if they were afraid, maybe cowered behind legs. This one—Bunji—did neither. She simply stood, totally passive. But she looked at Alice. Just looked.

And Alice looked back. Moments passed. Nothing was said. And then he realised Alice's question had gone unanswered. *Would she only be here for a week?*

Up to him.

'She's here for as long as you want her to be

here,' he said, a bit gruffly because for some reason the words were hard to say.

'But you said… Aunt Beatrice said… I'll have to go away.'

'If you like…if you end up caring for her then she can stay with you.' Why had he said that? Didn't he have plans to send this kid to boarding school? But the words had been said now, and they couldn't be unsaid. And he glanced at Kiara and caught a look of approval.

Wow.

What was it in that look?

Up until now her approach seemed to have been pure belligerence—even judgement. Well, so what? He had enough on his plate without worrying about what this slip of a vet thought of him. She was here at Beatrice's bidding. She was nothing to do with him, and what she thought of him was totally immaterial. But now…that one glance, quickly hidden, sent something fast and warm, something he had no hope of understanding. But as he turned back to focus on Alice and the dog, the look stayed with him.

'I don't know how to care for her,' Alice was whispering. To his amazement she'd dropped to her knees so she could look at the dog face to face. Kiara's hand was still on the dog's head, but he had the feeling it was more to reassure the dog than to protect Alice.

'That's why I'm here,' Kiara said, briskly now, and she squatted down as well. 'Your aunt Beatrice and uncle Bryn have paid me to come for a week, to help you learn to look after her. She'll take a lot of caring for, though, Alice. It's weeks since we found her and she's starting to recover, but she'll still take a long time to heal. And that's just her body. She's never been taught that she can trust. It'd be up to you to teach her that she can trust you as her friend.'

'But you'll go away.'

Dammit, he felt like an outsider. They were crouched, Kiara and Alice, with the dog between them. He stood above them and he felt…yes, outside.

Well, he couldn't crouch if he wanted to, he thought harshly. This damned knee… He'd smashed it completely. What he had now was a mechanical replacement, and the rest of his body was taking its own sweet time coming to terms with it. He was no longer in a wheelchair, but he needed his sticks and if he crouched…he'd have to ask Kiara to help him back up.

She'd do it. That was her obvious forte, helping wounded creatures. He was dammed if he'd be included in the list.

'I will go away.' Kiara was answering softly. 'Alice, I'm a vet. I run an animal refuge called

Two Tails, and my job is to help animals like Bunji.'

'My uncle and aunt are paying you to stay here?'

Spot on, Bryn thought. This kid was accustomed to hired help. It wouldn't help if she got to think of Kiara as anything else.

'My animal refuge is in trouble,' Kiara told her. 'Our buildings are starting to fall down. Your aunt and uncle have offered to help me fix things, which is how I got to meet you. So yes, I will be leaving after a week. I have to go back to Two Tails, but if you decide to keep Bunji then I'll keep checking and checking. And every time you need to talk about her then you can phone me straight away.'

And there it was, a direct, uncomplicated offer of friendship.

What was it in that offer that made him draw in his breath?

It also made Alice stare at Kiara for a long, long moment, almost as if she didn't believe, and she was searching in Kiara's face for the truth.

Kiara held her gaze, and for some reason to Bryn it felt as if the world were holding its breath.

And in the end it was Bunji who ended the impasse. She'd been standing unmoving between woman and child. Like a dog who'd been waiting for a very long time and was expecting to do more of the same. But for whatever reason, she suddenly decided on action.

She took a tentative step forward, just the one, but it was enough to put her almost nose to nose with Alice. Then, cautiously, as if she was expecting a rebuff, she lifted a paw.

Alice looked down at it. Almost as tentatively she put her own hand out and the dog's paw rested on it.

'She's very hurt?' she whispered, so softly Bryn could hardly hear.

'She is. She's healing though, and now she needs a friend, very badly.' Kiara's response was almost as soft.

'And you'll tell me what to do?'

'That part's easy,' Kiara told her. 'But what Bunji needs more than anything else is the promise that people won't let her down.'

'I won't let her down.'

'You'll be her friend?'

'I'll… I'll try.'

'Then that's a start,' Kiara said and grinned. She rose then, and smiled up at him, seriousness put aside for the moment. Her smile seemed wide and happy, and it leaped out and seemed to grab him in some way he couldn't explain. She was smiling straight at him, and that smile…

He'd thought she was plain. Suddenly she seemed anything but.

'This is indeed an excellent start,' she said, and put her hands together and raised them, a gesture of triumph. 'What do you say, Dr Dalton?'

'Bryn,' he said faintly.

'Bryn, then,' she agreed happily. 'Right, can you show me to my quarters? Alice, it's time we got on with it. You and Bunji have a whole lot of getting to know each other to do.'

CHAPTER FIVE

He hardly saw them for the rest of the day.

Oh, he stayed around to make sure Alice was safe. His housekeeper, for some reason looking almost rigid with disapproval, showed Kiara to her room—at the other end of the house from his. The dog followed beside her, pressed against her leg, and Alice trailed after, a shadow, ten feet away. Watching from the sidelines.

They ate lunch together. Kiara made small talk, bubbly nothings about his gorgeous house, the swimming pool… Was it heated? Did Alice swim? Did she think they might eventually teach Bunji to swim?

Alice either didn't respond or did so in monosyllables. Yes, no. That was her way. After all those words at the front door, she'd retreated.

Bunji lay under Kiara's chair, pressed against her leg. Not moving more than she had to. Every now and then he saw Kiara's hand slip down to pat the dog's ears.

The housekeeper came and went—a sniff or two to show her displeasure at a dog being inside her pristine house—but, dammit, this was his house.

And then he thought, was it? All the time he'd lived here, it was his succession of agency housekeepers who'd made the decisions on how to treat it. There'd been an architect first, then an interior designer, then gardeners and housekeepers.

He was surrounded by competence and cleanliness. Up until now, no dog would have dared show its face.

'Where will Bunji sleep?'

It was a whisper of a query, made as Alice pushed her half-eaten meal back. He'd expected her standard 'Please may I leave the table?' which was what he always got, almost as soon as she sat down. Surely this had to be an improvement.

'She can sleep by my bed,' Kiara told her. 'Until she wants to sleep by yours. That is, if you want her to. Would you like her to?'

'Dogs sleep outside.' It was a snap, coming from the middle-aged woman who was clearing the plates. She'd been sniffing her disapproval ever since Bunji had entered the house.

'Then I guess I sleep outside, too,' Kiara said, unblinkingly cheerful. 'Do you guys have a tent?'

'A tent?' Alice was clearly taken aback.

'You know, one of those canvas shelters you sleep in outside. It's called camping. It looks like it'll be warm tonight. We could set it up on the front lawn. It'd be fun.'

'The dog sleeps inside,' Bryn growled, and was he imagining it or did Alice's face fall a little?

'I'm allergic.' The housekeeper ceased clearing and crossed her arms in a stance that could only be called belligerent. 'It's already making my eyes run. I'm sorry, but enough. Either the dog stays outside, or I leave.'

There was a challenge.

If there was one thing Dr Bryn Dalton valued above all others it was order. He'd valued it before Skye and her daughter had arrived and thrown his life into chaos, and since then it had been the one thing he'd held to. Routine. Control.

Mrs Hollingwood had been with him now for over twelve months and he valued her. His meals arrived on time. His home was spotless. His possessions were never messed with. She'd seamlessly taken on Alice's care, making sure she was fed and clean, bringing out the useless games he'd purchased at the recommendation of the psychologists, clearing them away when it became clear Alice wasn't interested.

She was probably the best of the housekeepers he'd had, and she was now standing with her chest thrust forward, a line in the sand. The dog or me.

'There's plenty more jobs I can get through the agency,' she told him, and she thought she had him over a barrel. She knew his love of order. Her frustration had matched his the day his wheelchair had crunched over something Alice had left on his Italian mosaic floor and irreparably marked it. Mrs Hollingwood had cleaned it noisily, hmphing her displeasure.

And now...his perfect housekeeper was prepared to walk away because of a dog?

'She won't make a mess,' Alice said in a small voice.

'It'll shed,' the woman said, and jutted her bosom out still further. 'And look at those sores. You can't tell me that's hygienic.'

'Tents don't cost much,' Kiara said, semi-helpfully, from the other end of the table, and he glanced at her and thought—was she laughing? 'I have one back at Two Tails. If it's just for the week I can go home and fetch it, if you like.'

'Can I sleep in the tent, too?' Alice asked.

Oh, for heaven's sake... 'I'm sorry,' he said, definitely. 'But, Mrs Hollingwood, I'm afraid the dog stays, and it stays inside.'

Her face puckered, prune like. 'You won't get another housekeeper at short notice.'

There was a moment's silence. Something had

to give, but by the look on Mrs Hollingwood's face, it wasn't going to be her.

The dog or the housekeeper…

'Why do you need a housekeeper?' Kiara said at last, head cocked to one side as if interested in something she didn't understand.

'Don't be ridiculous. I can hardly cook and clean.'

She looked at him for a long moment, glanced at his walking sticks leaning against his chair, and nodded.

'Fair enough, but Alice and I can. That might give you time to find someone else.'

'My niece isn't here to be a drudge.'

'A drudge?' Her brows rose. 'Cleaning and cooking? That's hardly fair on Mrs Hollingwood.'

Uh-oh. Somehow he'd thrown petrol onto the fire and, predictably, it flared.

'I'm not a drudge,' the woman snapped. 'Don't you dare talk to me like that.'

'I'm sorry,' he said, appalled. 'I didn't mean…'

'But I won't work with the dog here. I mean, maybe one of those cute ones that don't shed, but not this one. This dog's disgusting.'

Alice had stood up. Now she moved, almost imperceptibly, to stand by Kiara's chair. 'I can learn to cook,' she said, and it was a frightened quaver, but her chin jutted a little.

'Hey, I can cook eggs,' Kiara said brightly. 'I can do 'em three ways, boiled, fried, poached. Though,' she admitted thoughtfully, 'sometimes my poached don't work too well. I watched a video on putting them in water after you've made the water twirl—you know, like going in circles down the bath plug. All that happened was I got twirly strings of egg. I had to get them out with a strainer. They tasted good on toast though. Hey, Alice, I can make toast, too.'

'Me, too,' Alice said, a bit more firmly.

And then, to his amazement, Kiara put up her hand and grinned. 'Snap. High five! We're home and hosed in the cooking department.'

And what was even more astonishing was that his little niece looked up at her upraised hand and smiled—she actually smiled!—and she high-fived in response.

Was that the first smile he'd ever seen from her? The first chink in her stoic impassivity?

Whatever, he felt like high-fiving himself. He needed a photo to send to Beatrice.

He needed Kiara to stay. Which meant…

'I'm sorry, Mrs Hollingwood, but if you can't stay with Kiara and her dog then we'll have to terminate,' he said gently. 'I'll organise terms with the agency.'

'You'll never get anyone else at this short notice.'

'Then stringy eggs it is, I guess,' he said, not taking his eyes from his niece. Unless it was to look at the chuckling woman who was now grinning at Alice as if she knew what a wonder she'd just achieved.

This woman was used to healing wounded creatures, he thought, and maybe, just maybe, her skills could be used to bring some joy to Alice.

He watched her for a moment longer and the thought flashed stupidly through his mind... Maybe she could bring some joy into his life as well?

Well, there was a stupid thought. Yes, he'd been wounded but only physically. His leg was healing. Soon he'd be back to normal—he'd have his life back to where he wanted it.

He could go back to having a decent housekeeper who kept his ordered world in the state he liked it. He could return to work with colleagues who shared his passion for state-of-the-art medical technology.

He could return to dating the women who understood his world, who didn't mess with his boundaries.

This woman was here for his niece. He might have to put up with stringy eggs for a while—and a shedding dog for a while longer—but she was a paid employee, here to do a job.

And that was it.

* * *

He excused himself and returned to his study as soon as lunch was done. Mrs Hollingwood was noisily clearing in the kitchen—'I'll wash up and then I'm done,' she'd snapped, and the noise she was making made the whole house aware of how angry she was.

She did have her reasons, he conceded. Drudge had been an insulting word. He'd tried to apologise but she was having none of it.

'You've said it, you'll pay,' she'd sniffed, and when he rang the agency to try and find a replacement, he found she'd got in before him.

'You've insulted one of our best workers,' he was told. 'And childminding was never on your list of requirements when you engaged her. Our staff is pressed to the limit. With what's happened I'm afraid you'll go well down the list. We'll let you know when we have anyone available.'

He made another couple of calls to alternative places but no luck.

So he had a gammy leg, a kid, a dog and a vet. He had no help.

But in a way he did. He glanced out of his window and saw Kiara and Alice had settled on the lawn, under the shade of a gorgeous flowering jacaranda. The dog was lying stretched out in front of them. Kiara seemed to be talking, but not

much. He couldn't see any response from Alice, but while he watched, her hand tentatively came out and stroked the dog's flank. A tiny stroke, almost immediately pulling back.

Kiara didn't seem to notice, was making no comment. She lay back and put her hands under her head, looking up through the dappling leaves. Sunlight was filtering through. While he watched, one of a drift of soft purple flowers disengaged from its branches and wafted down to land on her face.

She lifted it up and put it to her nose, and then smiled. And gently put the flower on the grass about three inches from Bunji's nose.

For some reason he found he was holding his breath.

There was a long pause while the dog didn't move and neither did Alice or Bunji. And then, almost at the same instant, the injured dog stretched forward a little—and right at that moment Alice leant over and put her nose on the bloom.

Noses touched.

They stayed, just like that, noses touching, for a long, long moment. Kiara didn't say a word, she just lay and watched.

This time he was sure it wasn't just him who was holding his breath. Maybe it *was* the whole world?

And then finally Alice lifted her head. Her hand came out and fondled the dog's uninjured ear. Her face turned up to Kiara's and she…

Giggled.

Oh, my…

High fives were never enough. Why did he feel like crying?

He had a student's PhD thesis on his desk. The 'Study of Neurological Problems After Heart Surgery' had some dubious sections—he needed to check references. He also had housekeeper problems.

Instead, he sat by the window and watched a kid watch a dog.

And watched a woman perform miracles?

They ate pizzas. Ordered in. Compared to the healthy food Mrs Hollingwood had been serving up, it left a lot to be desired. It couldn't last—he needed to find a cook or at least discover a healthy order-in source—but, watching Alice eat, he couldn't feel all bad.

Because she did eat. Bunji was stretched out on her dog bed, which Alice had set up beside her own chair. Kiara had said it was fine for Bunji to lie on the floor, but Alice had defiantly gone and fetched a blanket from her own bed. They'd compromised by lugging Bunji's big

cocoon bed into the kitchen. 'I guess it can go wherever Bunji goes for a while,' Kiara had said.

'Do you always provide such a bed for your clients?' Bryn asked, trying not to let Alice see him watching her. Was she really eating her third slice?

'Bunji's special,' Kiara said blithely. She was on her third slice, too. He'd ordered big, thinking it could be reheated for lunch tomorrow, but he obviously had another think coming. 'Besides, if you decide to keep her, it goes on your account.'

He blinked. Kiara grinned happily at him and kept on munching.

She really was extraordinary.

'So, I read about you on the Internet,' she said, and he nodded, torn between watching her and watching his niece. 'You're a doctor.'

'I am.' Cautious.

'That's excellent, because for the next few days I could use an assistant. I guess if you have qualifications, you might just do.'

And there was another blink. He might just… do?

'Um…thank you,' he said, cautiously. 'I might just…do what?'

'You can see the dressing on Bunji's thigh?' She motioned down. The dog's wounds were in various stages of healing but there was still a pad over her left hind thigh. Nothing else was covered.

'I wondered,' he said. 'Why isn't she wearing a cone?' He'd seen dogs before, friends' dogs, recovering from surgery and wearing wide plastic cones to stop them ripping at dressings.

'Because she has the sense to leave it alone,' Kiara said. 'Actually, we didn't have a choice. Her neck was so ulcerated we couldn't put anything on it. We sedated her for the first few days, but after that…it seems anything we do to her is okay with Bunji.'

'Her neck was sore?' Alice asked, looking down at the dog with concern.

'Her owners didn't check her collar,' Kiara told her. 'So when she grew, her collar got tighter and tighter.'

There was a silence while Alice thought this through.

Would he have told her that? Bryn wondered. Probably not. This kid had been through so much, she hardly needed more trauma. Alice ceased eating, then she put her hand down and tenderly stroked the dog's neck.

'I'm glad you have me,' she said, softly. 'I won't let you get hurt again.'

And there it was, an almost instant acceptance of ownership. Or responsibility.

Of connection.

Dammit, he was blinking again, and this time it wasn't through astonishment. Real men didn't cry. Like hell they don't, he thought savagely, and closed his eyes for a moment to give him time to pull himself together.

When he opened them, Kiara was watching thoughtfully. And was there a hint of laughter there as well?

'I guess I'll be billing you for the dog basket,' she said, and there it was. Definitely laughter.

This woman was unlike any woman he'd ever met before, plainly dressed, direct, and totally focused on her animals. She was here to get what she wanted—money for her shelter, a home for one of her strays.

What was it in her laughter that made him feel like joining in?

He managed a smile, but only just. He was suddenly feeling on shaky ground.

He wasn't accustomed to emotion. He wasn't accustomed to feeling how this woman made him feel.

No. It was the way the situation made him feel, he told himself harshly. Get a grip.

'Early days yet,' he growled.

'Yep,' she agreed cheerfully. 'You have a whole week to change your mind. Or Alice does.' But the appraising look she gave Alice—who'd returned to her pizza—also had a hint of smug.

'So meanwhile, can I take it that you'll accept the job as my medical assistant? Assuming, of course, that you don't faint at the sight of an open wound.'

'I'm a surgeon,' he said faintly.

'Yes, but my research says you're a professor in neurosurgery. What I know about neurosurgery is that it's pretty much all done with technology. Tiny cameras. Robotic stuff. Plus, you'd have nurses to clean up any mess. How long since you got your hands dirty, Dr Dalton?'

'I do work with trauma patients,' he said stiffly, though he had to admit, by the time he was called in the messy stuff had generally been dealt with.

'Well, that's a relief.'

'So what do you want me to do?'

'Help me change her dressing.'

'You need help with that?'

But he got a look then. A look that said back off.

'Alice, I'd like you to help me with most things for Bunji,' she said, talking to them both. 'If you're willing. But there's this one spot that needs your uncle's help. The sore on Bunji's leg needs cleaning every day, and Bunji wiggles. I need your uncle to hold her still. I do it first thing in the morning and last thing at night.'

'You mean…after I go to bed?' Alice asked.

'I guess,' Kiara told her. 'You probably go to bed earlier than we do. But…' She hesitated. 'It's up to you,' she told her. 'If your uncle says it's okay, then Bunji can be your dog now, and you can make the decisions. Is that okay with you, Dr Dalton?'

'Bryn,' he said, a bit too gruffly. Hell, where were these emotions coming from?

'Can Bunji be my dog?' Alice was all eyes.

So was Kiara. They were both looking at him, hopeful, expectant.

Even the dog was looking at him.

He thought suddenly of his sister, ten years older than him, bossy, gruff, overbearing. It was going to kill him to ring Beatrice and tell her she'd been right.

'Well?' Kiara said and her voice sounded almost teasing. Her laughter was insidious. He met her eyes, and he couldn't help smiling back.

And that smile… It felt as if something was cracking inside, something he didn't even know existed until now.

This was nonsense. It was emotional garbage, but Alice was waiting for an answer. They were all waiting for an answer.

'Fine,' he said, and he hadn't meant to sound quite as exasperated as he did. But he was feeling out of control, and control was something he valued above almost all else.

'If Dr Brail needs help, then I'll help her,' he told Alice. 'And if at the end of the week you still want her, yes, you can have her. Dr Brail will teach you all you need to know.'

'It's Kiara,' Kiara said gently and that smile softened.

But she was smiling at Alice, not at him. Her focus was all on the child. And the dog.

That was why she was here, he told himself. She needed to find this dog a home and earn money for her shelter. Then she'd be gone.

But why did he need to remind himself of that?

He didn't, he told himself. It didn't matter. *She* didn't matter.

She was a paid professional, here to do a job. She'd move on at the end of the week, leaving with the alacrity his housekeeper had just shown.

Leaving him with Alice.

That was what this was all about, he told himself, and no one could help him there. He needed to forge a relationship with a kid who needed… family?

If he could pay someone to fix that…

'So is it agreed?' Kiara asked, cutting across his thoughts, and he had to focus on here, on now. Where had this conversation started? Asking for help to change a dog's dressing?

'I can help,' he muttered and there was that flicker of amusement again.

'I *can* do it myself,' she told him. 'But it's so much better to work as a team. I'd imagine you'd find that in your working life, too, Dr Dalton.'

His working life. High-end neurosurgery. A team of brilliant clinicians, doctors, nurses, technicians.

'You know, I'm thinking one vet, one neurosurgeon and one little girl to love her, that's a force that might just make Bunji completely well again,' she told him, still smiling. 'So what do you say, team? Alice, are you in?'

'I'm part of a team?' Alice ventured, unsure.

'A Bunji-loving team,' Kiara said. 'What do you say?'

'I want to,' Alice whispered and then looked at Bryn. 'All of us?'

And what was a man to say to that? 'All of us,' he said weakly—and why did it suddenly feel like falling?

CHAPTER SIX

BEDTIME.

Every night since he'd been home from hospital Bryn had sat on Alice's bed and read her a story. That was what the psychologists had recommended. They'd given him a list of bland, non-threatening tales they said were designed to hold the traumatised Alice's interest just enough for her to drift into sleep, without the nightmares that trauma had burdened her with.

He never knew whether it worked with Alice. He suspected not. Every night she'd lain unmoving, politely waiting for him to finish, and when the last page was done, she'd turned her face against the wall and pulled the covers high. Hunching her shoulders. No hug required.

But tonight, after discussion that had itself amazed him, Kiara had set Bunji's bed beside Alice's. 'Your uncle and I will sneak in late and change her dressing,' Kiara had told her. 'Then I'll get up in the night and take her outside. And even if an accident happens—I guess it might as it's her first night in her new home—I'm your new housekeeper, right? I can cope with puddles.'

'You'd mop up wee?' Alice had asked, sounding awed.

'I'm a vet. I've mopped up a lot worse than that in my time.' Then Kiara had looked at the book Bryn had ready. 'This? Really? I like a book with a bit of action myself. Alice, how about if I tell you and your uncle about the time me and my friend Hazel rescued a whole bunch of poddy calves from drowning in a flood? With kayaks. Though my friend Hazel ended up swimming. You want to hear?'

Of course Alice did. And of course Bryn did. So he sat and listened and watched Alice's face.

She was entranced, and so was Bryn, and when the story ended and it was Kiara who tugged the covers up—did Alice really not flinch as Kiara gave her a kiss goodnight?—he was aware of a stab of loss that the story had ended.

'Right,' Kiara said briskly, the moment the door closed behind them, leaving child and dog to sleep. 'I have bookwork to do, and I need to ring Two Tails to find out how things are, so how about we convene in the laundry in an hour?'

'We can't do the dressing now?'

'The wound's still looking messy,' Kiara told

him. 'It was the worst of her wounds. It's healing now but she's still on antibiotics and I thought it'd be best if Alice didn't see under the pad for a few more days. So I thought it'd be best if we waited until Alice is asleep.'

'Why is it so bad?'

'Clostridial myositis,' she told him. 'I suspect that's the reason she was finally dumped—there's nothing like a smelly wound to make low lifers get rid of a problem the easiest way they know how. In this case dumping her near an animal shelter. You know clostridial myositis? It occurs in horses, pigs, dogs—bears, too, I hear—but it's as rare as hen's teeth. It's pretty much the same as clostridial myonecrosis—you may have heard of that as gas gangrene?—in humans. It was touch and go for the first few days, but I think I have it nailed now. I'd have liked to keep her at the shelter for another week for daily cleaning and dressing, but I only had this one chance to leave. So… See you in an hour, Dr Dalton?'

And without waiting for a response, she headed off, back to her part of the house. Brisk. Businesslike. Getting on with her life.

Which was what he needed to do.

He gazed after her for a moment, and then went back to his study.

But there was no way he could focus on the

finer points of checking the thesis he'd moved on to—'Cognitive Disturbances in Systemic Lupus Erythematosus'. Instead he found himself reading everything he didn't know about clostridial myositis.

An animal disease. An infection that left untreated meant certain death. Where treatment involved firstly skill to diagnose, including specific and expensive blood tests and scans. Then surgery. Then weeks of broad-spectrum antibiotics.

No wonder she was broke, he thought, stunned. To do this for a stray...?

Finally the hour was up. He emerged from his study to find Kiara bringing folded towels through the front door. 'What the...?'

'I brought my own,' she said, cheerfully. 'I had 'em in the car. I know, the gorgeous monogrammed pink things you've provided in my private bathroom would be marginally more comfortable for Bunji to lie on, but she's not all that fussy. Neither am I, come to think of it, but hey, I'm enjoying them and I'm not as likely to ooze as Bunji is.'

'Ugh,' he said faintly, and she grinned.

'Second thoughts, Dr Dalton? Do I need to keep smelling salts at hand?'

'Um...no,' he managed. 'But just how bad is it?'

'It's actually no longer likely to ooze,' she admitted. 'But the wound needs checking and it's not pretty. I could do it myself but it's easier with someone to hold her.'

He followed her as she headed for the laundry. Obviously she'd already sussed out her operating theatre—she'd cleared the massive granite bench and now she set the towels on its surface, her bag at the side. She spread a small sheet that had been wrapped in plastic, then set out businesslike tools. Surgeon preparing to operate?

'I wouldn't have brought her to you if I didn't think you'd have a fit, healthy Bunji by the time I left,' she told him, surveying her preparations with satisfaction. 'And I knew you were medical. There's still a chance that edges need debriding, which is why I have the gear. Your job is to hold and reassure. Not a lot of neurological skill involved, Dr Dalton, but maybe you can show off your skills some other time. Hang on while I fetch her.'

'I'll fetch her.'

'Yeah?' Her gaze moved from his face to the sticks he was still forced to use, and her brows raised in mild enquiry. Amusement? 'Will she leave a nice comfy bed to follow you? I don't think so. So you'll carry her?'

'I can.' He couldn't. He knew it but, dammit, he was disgusted with himself. He felt humiliated, and to add insult to injury she had the temerity to pat his shoulder.

'It's okay,' she told him kindly. 'You and Bunji will both be better soon. You can spread out the towels while I carry her.'

'Kiara...'

'Yes?' She gazed up at him and her eyes were twinkling. Teasing? The way she'd said *'You can spread out the towels...'* It was as if she were offering a treat to a three-year-old.

'I am competent,' he growled.

'I'm sure you are.' There was that smile again. 'Or you will be. You and Alice and Bunji... It seems I have a week to fix you all.'

And for some reason that silenced him.

She was just talking of his leg. Of course she was. She had no idea that ever since Skye's death he'd been feeling almost as vulnerable as the little girl who'd been hurled into his care. Which was stupid.

His world was carefully constructed to keep him in control, to block out the need for personal connection. His cold and solitary childhood had left him with a lifelong aversion to any kind of attachment. Now he had great friends, an awesome career, a magnificent home...

It was only the advent into his life of one small child that had tossed him into a sea of uncharted emotions.

The answer of course was for Alice to learn self-reliance. As he had. Then they could both move on.

So...self-reliance. Emotional safety.

Why did the arrival of this bouncy, impertinent vet seem to threaten it?

And then she was back, Bunji cradled in her arms, legs up. The dog's eyes were wide, but she was looking up at Kiara with complete trust.

Which meant a heart lurch—which was stupid.

He did *not* need to get personally involved. Or at least...okay, he did need to stay involved with Alice. Maybe even with this dog. But not with this woman.

His towels were laid out—at least he was that competent. Kiara laid the dog gently down.

'There you go, girl. Dr Dalton's assisting tonight and I've checked his medical credentials. Awesome. I bet he charges a mint, but add it to his account, not mine. Now, Dr Dalton is going to hold you steady and chat to you while I check out your leg.'

'Wouldn't it be better the other way around?' he asked. Kiara was surely the best placed to reassure, while checking a healing wound seemed simple.

But the look she gave him put him right back in his place. 'Hey, I might have checked your credentials online, but I'd need personal references to let you treat.'

'You're doubting…'

'Would you let me operate in your theatre without checking every facet of my qualifications? No? There you go, then. I'm very sure you're supremely qualified at what you do but this isn't something simple like brain surgery.' And she grinned, lifted his hand and placed it on Bunji's head. 'So accept your role, please,' she said. 'Words of reassurance, Dr Dalton. After all, you're Bunji's family from now on. It's time you two got acquainted.'

The man looked stunned. What was it with this guy? Kiara thought as she worked. He was acting almost as if he was afraid. But he did what he was asked. He stroked Bunji gently behind the ears, he spoke softly, and Bunji accepted him as someone who cared.

Did he care? This was such a strange situation—a brilliant surgeon with injuries, with a lonely, traumatised little girl. The two of them seemed as if they needed therapy. What they had was a vet and an already traumatised dog.

But something seemed to be happening. Maybe Beatrice had been right, she thought as she removed the dog's dressing. Alice's reaction to Bunji had seemed almost miraculous. And this guy… He'd been cold, aloof, but the way he was speaking to the dog…

'Tell me her medical history?' he said softly, in the same voice he'd been using to calm Bunji. She was carefully cleaning and checking the edges of the almost healed wound. It still took caution—the last thing Bunji needed was further infection.

'What you see is pretty much what we got,' she said, concentrating on what she was doing. 'You're looking at massive trauma—only that trauma's occurred since puppyhood. She's about a year old now. She's been severely malnourished and mistreated. The worst thing was the clostridium, but in a way it probably saved her life—the smell probably made whoever owned her get rid of her.'

'So…treatment?'

'First we had to figure what the problem was—I suspected, but there were so many other things going on and confirmation took time. The infection was well into deep tissue, and she was severely ill. The surgery on such a malnourished dog was tricky. After that…broad spectrum antibiotics, debridement, debridement, debridement. She may be left with a limp, but we're hopeful she won't. She's young. All she needs to do now is forget how much it hurt when she tried to use it.'

She finished what she was doing and reached for the antiseptic ointment. 'I guess…that's what you hope for Alice as well,' she said cautiously, without looking up. 'All she needs to do is forget past hurts. But how possible is that? Her trauma must be bone deep.'

'As you say,' he said curtly, and she did glance up then.

'And you, too,' she said, much more gently. 'There are hurts worse than physical pain. You lost your sister. I'm so sorry.'

'I hardly knew her.'

'But she was still your sister. I gather Beatrice hardly knows you, either, but she cared enough to leave her horses and her dogs to do what she could. That seemed quite some sacrifice. She must love you.'

'No one in my family loves anyone.'

'Really?'

There was a moment's silence at that, while she focused on what she was doing, and he regrouped. She'd pushed into places she had no right to push.

'So what about you?' he asked at last, and he knew he sounded defensive. Even a bit combative. Well, maybe he had the right.

'My grandma loved me,' she said, and she sounded defiant.

'Not your parents?'

She cast him another quick glance, as if she acknowledged that this was none of his business. Then, almost to his surprise, she responded. She spoke absently while she worked, as if it were a story about someone else.

'My dad's an egoist and a bully,' she said bluntly. 'He runs a big cattle property inland, but he treats cattle like objects, not creatures who need compassion. It seems he treated my mum the same way. She was good-looking and attracted him at a time when he'd decided he needed a wife. But he didn't want a partner. He needed a housekeeper and he needed sex. He also needed a son. I arrived after three miscarriages, and from them on I can only imagine how Mum was treated. She walked out when I was six—or maybe she ran. Heaven knows how broken she was. We don't know where she went but a couple of years later the police told us she'd died. Dad got himself another wife, and then another, but still no sons. However, I was a possession. *His.* Grandma wanted me, but she wasn't allowed to have me. When Dad was away I got to stay with her, though. Grandma's home was my refuge and now it's an animal refuge. Two Tails. I love it.'

'So parents...'

'I decided I didn't need 'em,' she said curtly. 'But I do need someone. Grandma was my someone. As I guess—I hope—you'll be Alice's someone. Maybe she'll be yours.'

'I don't need…someone.'

'Everyone does,' she said simply, and went back to applying a new dressing. 'That's it, then. I reckon a week and this pup will be right as rain, ready to start her new life. A life where someone cares. You will care, won't you, Dr Dalton?'

'Bryn,' he said, sounding goaded. 'And yes, I'll care.'

'For Bunji and for Alice.'

'Butt out,' he growled, and she did, but she ventured one last smile.

'I think it's wonderful,' she said simply. 'Your sister says you're a loner, Dr Dalton. Well, not any more you're not. You have Alice, and now you have Bunji, and I have every hope in the world that you'll end up like Grandma and me. A family.'

A family.

With the dog safely treated and seemingly settled beside Alice's bed again—Alice's bedroom was right next to his and with both the doors open he could hear if there was trouble—he was free to sleep.

He couldn't.

Of course he couldn't. He'd hardly slept since the accident.

His leg ached—no, make that hurt. The surgery had been extensive. It'd hurt for months. He could use drugs—they'd make him sleep as well as ease the pain—but since Beatrice had left, he was the only one in the house with Alice. And she had nightmares.

He had to be there for her.

Family.

Kiara's words kept playing over and over in his head. *'I have every hope in the world that you'll end up...a family.'*

It had already happened, he thought savagely. He had no choice.

When Skye had brought her daughter here, demanding he take care of her, he'd reacted with incredulity. He'd had no intention of being a hands-on uncle, much less a father figure. He wasn't the least sure he had the emotional depth for anyone to depend on him.

But this woman—Kiara—seemed to have emotional depth in spades. She seemed to know how to talk to Alice, how to draw a solitary, damaged child out of her shell. She was warm, kind—loving?

That was who Alice needed, not someone who'd never figured out what loving was.

He could learn?

But it wasn't something learned—he had the intelligence to figure that out. It was something instilled from childhood, the ability to give and receive affection.

Kiara's grandmother must have been quite some woman, he thought. Somehow she'd figured it out.

Could he?

You can't teach an old dog new tricks. For some reason the phrase came into his mind and stuck.

Hell, he was only thirty-seven.

Yeah, but how did you learn to love?

By feeling for Alice? The child's plight had gutted him. He was prepared to do whatever it took to make her happy—even taking on a dog. Even maybe keeping her here in this house, not sending her to boarding school. The plan to send her to boarding school had now been complicated by letting Kiara load her with the dog. Maybe he could send her to the local school, pay other parents to involve her in after-school activities, pay a nanny.

As his parents had done? Yeah, as if that had worked.

But the alternative? One of the shrinks he'd talked to had suggested—tentatively—that he might cut back on work, be a sort of part-time parent.

And do what? Be there at the school gate, walk her home every night?

His work was his life.

This was doing his head in. He had not a single clue what the future held. The only thing he could focus on was getting his leg healed, getting back to work, getting back to some kind of normal.

Which right now meant figuring out how to get to sleep.

Which meant not lying staring at the ceiling thinking of a slip of a kid, a vet, looking at him and saying…

'I have every hope in the world that you'll end up...a family.'

And at the other end of the house—in what the housekeeper had brusquely described as the guest wing—Kiara was also wide awake.

Thinking of a wounded kid. A wounded dog.

A wounded man?

What was it about him that had got under her skin?

The first time she'd met him she'd actively disliked him. Oh, sure, she'd felt sorry for his situation, but he'd been arrogant, wanting to throw money at a problem that any idiot could see money couldn't cure.

But watching him tonight… While she'd related the story of rescuing the poddy calves, while she'd embellished the story to entrance a sleepy child, while she'd tried to make Alice smile…she'd glanced up at him and seen…what could almost be imagined as hunger.

As if he was as desperate for a world he could escape into as Alice was.

Well, she was only going to be telling stories for a week, she told herself briskly. He'd have to figure a way to tell them himself.

Why did that make her feel suddenly desolate?

Stop it, she told herself harshly. She had enough to feel desolate about without adding Dr Bryn Dalton and his niece to her list.

Go to sleep.

But sleep was evasive. Finally she flicked on her bedside light and propped herself on pillows. A bit of Internet drifting, she thought. Puppies. Reruns of silly bits from movies. Something to turn her mind from where it kept heading.

To the man sleeping at the other end of the house.

And almost unconsciously she found herself typing his name into a search engine, looking not for professional qualifications but for media reporting of Skye's death.

And here it was.

Heroic Doctor Saves Child from Local Cliffs!

At three this morning a woman's body was retrieved from the rocks directly under the notorious cliffs near Clovelly. The woman was thought to have fallen from above. A child, believed to be the woman's daughter, appears to have tried to climb down after her, but fell herself. It seems she was trapped on a ledge almost at water level, with bad weather, heavy seas and a rising tide.

This set the scene for what police say was an extraordinary rescue.

A Clovelly resident, reportedly Dr Bryn Dalton, an eminent neurosurgeon at nearby Sydney Central hospital, was first on the scene. With the child in danger of being washed off the ledge, he managed to crawl down the cliffs to reach her.

Police say he had almost made it before the cliff face crumbled. He somehow still reached the child, and managed to cling to her until emergency services were able to retrieve them—a process that took almost an hour while waves constantly washed over the pair.

The child was lifted by rescue services, seemingly unhurt, and has been taken to Sydney Central for observation. Dr Bryn Dalton has been admitted to Sydney Central with serious leg injuries but is expected to make a full recovery.

Early reports say the woman's body was found wedged between rocks under water.

It is not known at this time what relationship, if any, exists between Dr Dalton and the pair he attempted to rescue, but police are recommending he be referred for consideration for Australian's highest award for acts of conspicuous courage, the Cross of Valour.

This broadsheet can only agree.

Me, too, Kiara thought as she read and reread the article. She definitely agreed. The cliffs around here were notorious. To climb down them was impossibly dangerous and, living here, he must know the risks.

But then her attention was drawn back to the screen. The next Internet feed had followed automatically. Instead of a written report, it was a video, obviously filmed by a media channel chasing the rescue chopper.

Kiara never looked at these sorts of scenes. They mostly seemed a voyeuristic intrusion on what must be an appalling enough trauma for those involved, without seeing endless replays in full technicolour.

This time she couldn't look away.

The rescue was filmed in darkness—of course—but the scene was lit by the massive floodlights beaming from the rescue chopper. She could see the maelstrom of breaking waves, flattened a little by the massive whirring of the chopper blades.

It had been pouring with rain, and the wind looked fierce. It must have been dangerous for the chopper, much less for the people on the cliff.

She watched, caught, seeing the initial sweep of the chopper, the storm-tossed seas, the bottom of the cliffs.

A hesitation, a shift of the chopper from its sweep path.

Then figures huddled on a ledge, not even clear of the breaking waves. A man, lying on the ledge, his back to the water. The waves crashing over him.

The chopper rising, obviously to try and get a better view.

A glimpse of the child spooned against the man's chest, his arms fiercely wrapped, holding her, using his body to protect her against the force of the sea.

She watched in sickening fascination as the chopper steadied or tried to steady against the wind. Waited, obviously hoping against hope for the wind to die.

Then a lone figure—another hero, Kiara thought—was being lowered down, a stretcher with him. He was using the stretcher as armour against the cliff face.

She saw Bryn turning, holding the child up. Another wave crashing over them. How did he keep his hold?

She saw the stretcher man waiting, watching the sea. Then a break… Steady, sure hands, fastening Alice. Bryn, his body wedged between rocks to hold him as safe as such a tenuous hold could make him, helping secure his niece.

Alice clinging. And Bryn… At the last minute, there was a fierce hug, then he released his hold on the rocks so that momentarily his hands held her face. Words, unheard and yet obvious, the care was unmistakeable.

The love?

And then the rising of the stretcher and Alice was safe.

What followed was an interminable wait while Alice was pulled into the chopper and the camera abandoned Bryn. Then the return to retrieve him.

She saw the moment stretcher man realised the extent of the damage to Bryn's leg. As he pulled out from his crammed position, even with the grainy image she could see its grotesque break.

There was no time for bracing it, though. With the rising tide there was no time for anything. He was almost roughly hauled onto the stretcher.

It's a wonder he didn't pass out from the pain, she thought, but at least he was safe.

At least the little niece he'd saved was safe.

He must love her.

Yeah, but he doesn't know it, she thought. Or maybe he does but he's not admitting it.

She thought back to Beatrice's words at that first meeting. *'A stupid act of bravado caused by his failure to wait for the proper emergency services.'*

She had no doubt what the outcome would have been if Bryn hadn't performed that *'stupid act of bravado'*.

Dear heaven…

She flicked off the light, but the images from the news reports were too vivid, too awful. A little girl, whose mother was lost.

Okay, she couldn't help herself. She'd just check on Bunji, she told herself, and she slipped out of bed, poked her toes into her shabby slippers—she really should have supplied herself with new ones to fit into this fancy house—and padded through the darkened house to Alice's room.

And stopped short at the open door.

Alice was in bed, curled under the blankets, the night light showing a child fast asleep. Her fine blonde hair was splayed around her on the pillow. Her face was still far too pale.

One of her skinny arms was hanging down. Her hand was resting on Bunji's coat.

Bunji was in the cocoon of a dog bed, and beside the cocoon…

Bryn.

He was sitting on the floor, his bad leg stiffly out before him. He, too, had his hand on Bunji's coat, as if to say, okay, girl, I might have woken you, but I mean you no harm.

He was watching both girl and dog.

Kiara stood in the doorway, and suddenly another memory came, unbidden.

She'd been ten years old. Midsummer on her father's farm, she'd been an unsupervised child playing in a field of uncut hay. Then, she'd come across a tiger snake—one of Australia's most venomous. It had taken her twenty minutes to get back to the house, and by the time she did the venom had taken hold.

Her father hadn't wanted the bother of nursing a child, so three days later her grandma had picked her up from hospital. Home she'd gone with Grandma. That night… In the small hours she'd stirred and found her grandmother sitting beside her bed. Just sitting, which seemed astounding all by itself. She could never remember her grandma's knitting needles being still, but that night they had been.

'I'm just watching,' the elderly lady had said

as she'd stirred. She'd put her hand on Kiara's face and then leant over and kissed her. 'I'm just watching you breathe, Kiara, my love. You go back to sleep. Your breathing's safe with me.'

And she had. She'd remembered the fear and pain of the snake bite, her father's disgust that she'd been so stupid, and he'd had to lose half a day's work. She remembered the loneliness of hospital where she'd understood little.

But mostly she remembered her grandma's hand and the kiss. *'Your breathing's safe with me.'*

And now, without warning, her eyes started swimming with tears.

She backed away—there was no way she would interrupt such a scene—but she must have made some faint noise because Bryn saw her.

'Don't get up,' she whispered, but he already had, pushing himself to his feet—and that was pretty impressive for someone as injured as he was.

'Just checking,' he muttered. He was dressed in boxers and T-shirt—designer, she'd bet—but then who was looking at pyjamas? He'd caught the sticks beside the bed and limped out to the passage. 'I don't like the idea of the dog being with her. A strange dog...'

Liar, she thought. *There's no way you're worried about Alice's safety with Bunji.*

You were watching them both breathe.

'There's no risk,' she told him. They were outside the door now and could speak. Though he was a bit close.

Actually he was very close. She thought suddenly—she wouldn't mind another layer or two of clothing. She was wearing a skimpy nightgown and worn slippers.

It was crazy to be conscious of it—as if a guy like this would even look twice at someone like her—but even so, she wished she'd brought her nice thick woolly dressing gown.

It'd be crazy in this season, in this climate-controlled house, but she wanted it all the same.

Professional, she reminded herself. She was here in a professional capacity, so she had to act like it.

He was saying he was here because he was worrying about risk?

'I've had Bunji in care for days now,' she told him, still speaking softly, but having—stupidly—to focus on preventing the ridiculous way her voice wobbled. 'In that time she's been stressed, hurt, ill. I've had to give her injection after injection. I've had her on a drip, and I've had to keep sedation to a minimum because she was so weak. In all that time, no matter what I've had to do to her, she's never offered so much as a tiny growl. She's bombproof, Dr Dalton. Do you really think I'd expose Alice to risk?'

'And yet you came to check.'

'I'm here to do a medical check on my patient.' She assumed a tone of virtue. Thankfully she almost had her voice back to normal. 'You're paying for a veterinarian to stay here for a week. Nightly checks are part of my job.'

'So you're playing Florence Nightingale—the lady with the lamp.'

'There's no need for sarcasm.'

'Believe it or not, I didn't mean to sound sarcastic.'

'No? Well, thank you.' She glanced up at him and found he was looking at her strangely. Creature from Mars? Creature in flimsy nightie and shabby, fluffy slippers.

'If all's well here, then I'll go back to bed,' she told him.

'Kiara?'

'Yes?' Unconsciously she lifted her chin. Braced?

'Thank you,' he said.

'I…there's no need,' she managed at last. 'You're paying me, and this is my job.'

'Bunji's not just another dog, though, is she?'

'No,' she admitted. 'She's not.'

'Beatrice says you specialise in finding homes for dogs who are sometimes…less than desirable. Elderly dogs who'll cost heaps as they near the end of their lives. Dogs with problems. But thanks to you, Bunji is recovering to have no problems at all. A dog less than a year old? Bombproof, as you say? In another few weeks you could have sold her…

'Not for as much as you're paying.'

'Is that the only criteria for giving her to us?'

'No,' she admitted. 'I thought… Alice needs her.'

'And me?'

'I'm not going there.' She hesitated. 'But okay, I'll be honest. Bunji's got to me in a way few other dogs have. I've seen maltreated dogs, treated them, seen them successfully rehoused. But something about Bunji…' She took a deep breath.

'She's touched my heart,' she said, feeling self-conscious for saying such a thing, but she could think of no other way to put it. 'And in a way, Alice has done the same thing. And you. Your situation… So I thought… I hoped that you could all heal together. Yes, the money Beatrice is offering will help keep Two Tails going for another few months, but maybe the end of my refuge is inevitable. If Bunji doesn't fit here, if she doesn't get the love she deserves, and give the love she's capable of in return, then I'm taking her right back.'

'And why did you come to the other end of the house in the middle of the night?' he asked, and his voice sounded a bit strange. As if he was in uncharted territory?

'Because I like a happy ending,' she retorted. 'Or the prospect of the same. Because I suspect how much both Alice and Bunji need it and I'm aching for it to happen.'

'Because you care.'

'Is there anything wrong with that?'

'No,' he said, still in that curious voice. He was watching her, his dark eyes expressionless. Giving nothing away of what he was feeling.

Did he think she was stupid?

Well, maybe she was, she thought, and once more she was acutely aware of her faded nightie and her shabby slippers. And her bare legs and the fact that this was the middle of the night, and she was in this man's house and…and…

'I need to go back to bed,' she said, a bit too brusquely, and maybe he got her unease because he stood aside fast. Assuring her he meant no threat?

Which was crazy. No threat had been implied. But there was…something.

Some pull.

A man and a woman in not enough clothing, in the middle of the night? A guy who looked like Bryn Dalton?

Get over it, she told herself, and turned to leave.

'Kiara?'

'Yes?' But there was silence and finally she turned back to face him. 'Is there…is there something else?'

'Just…' The silence hung. Everything hung. She was waiting but she didn't know for what.

And finally he propped one of his sticks against the wall and lifted his hand, tentatively. If she wanted to—if her body was capable of moving—she could have stepped away, but she did no such thing. She simply stood and waited for what was to happen.

Which was little enough. His fingers reached her face. One long finger ran the length of her cheek. Lightly. A feather touch, that was all. And still those eyes remained…expressionless?

Or maybe not. Maybe there was a touch of tenderness…

And why she should suddenly think back to the moment Bunji had raised a paw… A connection?

Ridiculous. As he withdrew his hand and she took a step back, the thought disappeared.

'Goodnight, Kiara,' he said softly, and she managed a brusque nod.

'Goodnight, Dr Dalton.'

And she turned and fled.

* * *

Bryn should go to bed, too. Instead, he stood in the darkened passage and wondered what on earth had just happened.

He'd reached out and touched her.

Why? She was an employee, here to do a job. It was the middle of the night. Hell, she could just about have him up on an assault charge for what had just happened.

He hadn't held her.

He hadn't kissed her.

He'd wanted to.

What was it about her?

It was just the situation, he told himself. He was a man, she was a woman, there was chemistry.

She was beautiful.

But not in the way most of the women he knew were.

Not one of those women would be seen dead in what she was wearing tonight. And it wasn't just her nightwear. Her normal clothes were plain, serviceable, well worn. She wore her hair scraped back. No make-up.

The research he'd done on Two Tails had led to its website, where Kiara had included a brief summary of its proprietor's life. She'd been raised on a farm, somewhere in rural New South Wales, and she'd spent many of her holidays at her grandmother's home. She'd lived in central Sydney during her training, but the city wasn't her thing.

That was what she looked like—a woman who spent as much time as she could outdoors. And by the look of her hands, she spent much of that time working. Hard.

So what was making him stand in the dark and feel as if…he'd just touched something precious? Something quite, quite lovely?

He needed to get a grip, to refocus. He needed to get Alice sorted…

Get Alice and Bunji sorted.

There was an issue. Boarding school had seemed the best option but now… He wouldn't send Alice even if he could, he realised. He was becoming as emotional about this whole issue as Kiara.

And there he was, thinking of Kiara again. What was it about the woman that had him so unsettled?

Was it just that he'd been too alone for too long? He liked his solitude, but since his accident that solitude had been multiplied to the point where he saw Alice, he saw rehab staff and hardly anyone else. And now here was a woman he didn't know, but someone who cared, someone who'd come through a strange, darkened house to check on his niece and her dog.

Someone who had, in some small way, already eased his weight of responsibility.

So that was why he must be feeling like this, he told himself harshly. This was gratitude and relief. Nothing else was appropriate, so he needed to stop thinking about Dr Brail…as he was thinking. She was here for a week. She'd be working with Alice and Bunji and that was a great opportunity for him to get some work done.

Right. Go back to bed.

He went, but as he limped back to his room the thought of a woman stayed with him. A woman in a shabby nightgown, a woman who was nothing to do with his world, a woman who'd be gone in a week.

He'd get over it. He had enough academic work to last him for months. He could use this week to clear the backlog.

He could use this week to gather his independence once more—and in the process he could keep as far from Dr Kiara Brail as he could.

CHAPTER SEVEN

THE NEXT DAY saw Kiara and Alice spending almost all their time together. Alice was still aloof, still wary, but she was desperate to learn everything she could about her new pet and communicating with Kiara was a necessary evil to achieve it. Bunji was still attached to Kiara, where Bunji went, Alice followed, and they quickly became a pack. Kiara, Alice, Bunji.

Bryn wasn't part of it.

He appeared for lunch—the fridge and pantry were magnificently stocked, and Kiara did the basics. She was supposed to be here as a vet, she thought wryly, but for the money she was being paid a bit of basic housework seemed a reasonable inclusion. She hadn't expected to be left completely alone with child and dog, though, and was vaguely disturbed when, as soon as he finished lunch, he pleaded the need to work and headed back to his study.

He did the same at dinner. Kiara had whipped

up a basic pasta. He asked Alice if she'd prefer Kiara to read to her that night and Alice said a simple yes. So he disappeared again.

Kiara headed to her bedroom, tried to read and then tried to sleep. She did neither well.

The next day followed the same pattern.

So what? She was being paid, she told herself. Actually she was being overpaid—a lot—and what did it matter if Bryn kept to himself? In a way it even seemed a good idea.

The way he'd touched her had caused a frisson of sexual awareness that stayed with her, and in her bed that night there was a restlessness, as her mind wandered into a fantasy of what-ifs?

There'd been men in Kiara's life—of course there had—but they'd been fleeting. Her only experience of family had left her with no real desire to start one of her own and, besides, where would she find time? Her passion was Two Tails. It took all her energy, all her waking hours, and the thought of a lover…

A lover like Bryn…

Was impossible. Even if he was interested—which he wasn't.

But still there was this frisson of awareness, a heightening of senses that left her disturbed. This man seemed extraordinary. He was so aloof, so like a grown-up version of Alice, but underneath she could sense something more. A lot more. The feel of his fingers on her cheek… That touch… It had woken such feelings…

Which were useless and she had to keep them in check. The best way to keep them at bay was therefore to avoid him, so his distance was a good idea. For her.

But not for Alice.

As the days wore on she realised there were deeper issues at stake. Alice was starting to relax with her, even to chat, maybe even to think of her as a friend—and Alice needed a friend. Or more. Kiara knew from personal experience how vulnerable a lonely child could be, and she knew Alice was aching for someone to love. But that someone couldn't be her.

She was starting to wonder how sensible was it to encourage a solitary child like Alice to get close to her. She was here as a paid employee, but she was a vet, not a nanny, and soon she had to leave. She was no psychologist, but even she could see that if Alice and Bunji were to end up with a happy ever after, Bryn had to be included.

And finally, she called him on it.

Dinner had just ended. 'Will you tell me the story about the kayaks and the cows again tonight?' Alice asked shyly, and Kiara took a deep breath and shook her head.

'You know, I've been talking so much today that my throat's sore,' she told her. 'So tonight's my night off. I'm going to sit by the fire in the sitting room and rest my voice so I can talk to you tomorrow. Your uncle's on story duty tonight.'

'I have...' Bryn started but she flashed him such a look that he rethought. 'I guess I can,' he conceded. 'You choose a book.'

'I like real stories,' Alice whispered.

There was a moment's silence. Real stories. Stories where this man revealed something of himself. Kiara could almost see the armour he had in place. How much easier to read someone else's story?

She found she was holding her breath, waiting for him to refuse. His face was closed. Every instinct was to rush in, suggest, fix things, but she compressed her lips and held her thoughts in.

And finally, he cracked.

'I guess I could tell you about porriwiggles,' he said, almost as if the words were forced out of him.

'Porriwiggles?' Alice stared at him in confusion.

'Most people call them tadpoles,' he explained. 'Or baby frogs. When I was a boy, my father had a property with a dam in the home paddock. He used to send me and my nanny there when he was...when he wanted the city house to himself. Nanny taught me to catch porriwiggles—that's what she called them. We put them in tanks and watched them grow, and then put them back in the dam when they turned into frogs. But funny things happened to those porriwiggles—and to me, too, as I tried to catch them.' He thought for a moment. 'You know, your mom was older than me, and she'd gone to America by the time I was born, but she would have spent time on our dad's farm as well. I bet she would have caught porriwiggles.'

And he'd caught her. A story that included porriwiggles—and her mother. 'How…how did you catch them?' Alice whispered, and Bryn cast Kiara a goaded glance—an unspoken *What have you got me into?*—but then softened as he answered Alice.

'Let's get you to bed and I'll tell you,' he told her. 'We must give Dr Brail's voice a chance to recover, mustn't we? I've heard her yelling at you and at Bunji—wow, she's such a bossy teacher. You must be really scared of her.'

And Alice got up from the table, looked up at her uncle—and giggled.

Kiara sat by the fire in the sitting room, because she'd told Alice that was where she was going—and also it seemed somehow mean to disappear to her bedroom when she'd pushed him into taking charge. Plus, it was a gorgeous living room. The open fireplace was huge, surrounded by a magnificent marble surround. There were massive, down-filled settees—four of them—and in front of the fire was a vast wool rug, all colours, a rug so rich it looked as if it had just this minute arrived on the plane from Persia.

Alice thought briefly of the squashed, worn and slightly puppy-chewed rug in front of her fire back at Two Tails and almost grinned.

The fire had been set—probably thanks to Mrs Hollingwood. Kiara put a match to the kindling, and watched it grow into a truly wonderful fire, but as she watched her desire to smile faded.

She had a sudden urge to fetch Bunji to share. She couldn't. Bunji was Alice's dog now, but she needed a dog. She needed…someone?

If she lost Two Tails…

She'd never be without a dog, she told herself, or at least, not for long. Once she found herself a decent job and secure place to live, she'd be in the position to have another.

But right now, sitting by the fire, thinking of Bryn telling stories of porriwiggles to Alice, she was aware of a void that had nothing to do with dogs.

Family…

One day…

Really? She was thirty-two and she'd always been far too busy for serious relationships. And besides, she had no idea how they worked. To give your heart to a man…to surrender control as her mother had…the thought had always terrified her. She'd settled with herself that she'd be happy and safe with her cottage and her dogs. It was only now, when she was feeling as if she were being torn by both, that she was having these strange feelings.

The door opened and Bryn limped in. She should jump up, say goodnight, go, but he crossed the room and sank into the closest settee, as if he wanted to talk?

It would have seemed mean to flee. Sensible though, she thought. But mean.

'How did it go?'

'She liked the porriwiggles.'

'I imagine she would. She needs as many stories about her family as she can get.'

He cast her a strange look. 'I guess.'

'So…porriwiggles?' she asked, figuring that had to be a safe bet for conversation.

'I had a menagerie,' he told her. 'The ducks used to eat the frogspawn, so I figured I was saving lives by taking the spawn up to the stables and keeping it safe until they hatched and grew into frogs. I guess I didn't realise all I was doing was making ducks fatter by giving them a much bigger diet of froglets.'

She smiled. 'I hope you didn't tell Alice that.'

'No.' He shrugged. 'I told her the funny bits,

how I used an old bath as a boat to get to the island in the middle, how my bath floated away, and nanny had to wade in up to her armpits to rescue me. How I used old petrol cans to cart water from the dam to replace the water in my tanks—I learned the hard way that tap water has chlorine in it. And one day I remember thinking hey, this can is full already, I must have already filled it, so I tipped it in and it was petrol. I realised as soon as I smelled it. I remember flying into the kitchen and yelling at the cook that I needed the strainer, then tipping the whole tank through the sieve and washing and washing the little froglets in dam water. And the amazing thing was that they survived.' He shook his head. 'There's a veterinary miracle for you.'

'Amazing,' she said and grinned. 'I should write it up for *Aus Vet Monthly*.'

'It's copyright,' he told her, and he smiled back down at her.

And that smile…

Uh-oh. She had to get out of here. She rose, and he rose, too, and once again they were too close. How had that happened?

Maybe it just *seemed* too close. Maybe, the way she was feeling, half a room away would seem too close.

'I need to go to bed,' she said, a trifle unsteadily. 'I just stayed here to see how you went.'

'To check on me?' But he was still smiling.

'No!' She flushed. 'Sorry. It's none of my business.'

'But you did force me to read to her.'

She tilted her chin at that. 'It *is* none of my business,' she repeated. 'But I'm leaving soon and you're staying. She needs you to be her friend, not me.'

'I don't know how...'

'Then learn. Tonight was a great start.'

'You're the psychologist?'

'No,' she said, gently now. 'I'm an interested onlooker who has to move on. But you and Alice... I hope you'll be friends for life. You can do it. I know you can.'

And then, there was something about the way he was looking...something about his expression... Fear? Longing? Bewilderment? She couldn't figure it out, but somehow, before she could stop herself, before she even realised what a crazy thing it was to do, she stepped forward and rose on tiptoes. 'You'll be fine,' she said—and she kissed him.

It was a feather kiss, a brushing of lips on his cheek. It was a kiss of friendship, a kiss of warmth, a kiss of some deep recognition that this man was in as much need of human contact as his niece was. It had been entirely instinctive, and as soon as she'd done it she backed away. Horrified. She'd shocked herself. What was she thinking?

And he looked…as if he didn't know either. He put his hand to his cheek and looked at her. Just looked.

They were both in uncharted territory.

The silence stretched on. He raised a hand as if to reach out to her and then he paused and looked down at it—and so did she. They were on the edge of something…

Which was stupid and unprofessional and doomed to lead nowhere, she told herself, panicked. This man was a client, nothing more. She had only to glance around his amazing, over-the-top designer sitting room to see that he was a world away from her world. As her mother's world had been so far from her father's.

And she wasn't stupid. She was a vet, here on a job. She backed away, almost in fear, and her hands came up in an instinctive gesture of defence.

'I… I'm sorry,' she muttered. 'That was totally inappropriate. Goodnight, Bryn.'

And somehow, she managed to get her shocked body to move.

He didn't follow her as she fled. He didn't call after her.

He just stood in silence, for a very long time.

She'd performed a miracle. She and her blessed dog.

Bryn sat in his study, supposedly working.

They'd come to an arrangement. He now spent the mornings and the evenings with Alice. The afternoons, though, they'd decided, could be his. Kiara needed to train Bunji with Alice, and he really did need to work.

But increasingly he was finding it harder to concentrate. Right now, instead of focusing on notes on neural pathways, he was looking out over the lawn to where a child and a dog were tumbling down the grassy slope toward the swimming pool. For the last hour Kiara had been trying to teach Bunji—and Alice—to roll, using a pocket full of treats, laughter and pats. Finally she'd done it. Now child and dog were nose to nose, rolling down the slope as one.

Alice was squealing with delight.

Kiara was sitting at the top of the slope, beaming as if she'd been given the world.

He felt as if *he'd* been given the world. Alice was a child again.

What a gift.

But tomorrow Kiara was leaving.

The thought was like a storm cloud heading his way with frightening speed. But they'd be fine, he told himself, as he'd been telling himself for days. The way Alice felt about Kiara—and increasingly, the way he was starting to feel about Kiara—it wasn't practical or sensible to continue. He and Alice would figure out a new normal. Kiara been employed for a fixed time and that time was over. Alice had to learn independence.

They'd manage.

And then his phone rang.

The screen said the call was from Archie Cragg, the hospital's administrator. He and Archie had last talked just before Kiara had arrived. 'I'll be back as soon as Alice starts school,' Bryn had told him, and Archie had agreed.

'Take all the time you need,' he'd assured him, as he'd said all along. 'We want you back healthy, with things sorted at home.'

But now Archie's voice held a note of strain. 'Mate?' And instantly Bryn knew something was wrong.

'Problem?'

'You could say that,' Archie said grimly. 'We've lost Rod and Caroline.'

What the…?

Rod Breehaut was second in charge of Neurology—he'd taken charge while Bryn was off work. Rod was married to Caroline, who was also a neurologist.

Bryn, Rod and Caroline made up Sydney Central's quota of fully trained neurologists.

Not another accident, surely. His heart seemed to hit his boots, but Archie was still talking.

'It's a bit of an affair.' The voice on the end

of the line was tight with fury. 'It seems Rod's been having it off with one of our med students. A student! He knows the rules. He's fifty and she's twenty-two—poor kid, it's like she's star-struck. Her assessment's about to come up and he's her supervisor—can you imagine the situation that puts them both in? Anyway, Caroline caught them at it, in the staffroom of all places, and she screeched the place down. I've had to sack him on the spot, and now Caroline's decided to go home to her mother. Who lives in Birmingham! She leaves tomorrow. Bryn, I know I told you to take all the time you need, but you're pretty much recovered, right? Mate, we have patients in real trouble. We need you.'

She looked up and Bryn was limping across the lawn to join them. And her heart seemed to sort of...jolt.

Well, that was dumb, she told herself. Just because the man was too good-looking for his own good... Just because he was so darned sexy...

But it was more than that. Nothing had changed in the sexiness department since she'd first met him, but since the night she'd found him watching over his little niece, the way she'd felt about him had definitely changed. And after the night of...the kiss...she'd watched his interaction with Alice with a kind of wonder.

Until Bunji had broken through, uncle and niece had seemed tightly bound within themselves, shielding themselves from personal connection.

She watched him now and saw his face crease into a smile as wide as the one she'd felt when Bunji and Alice had finally nailed their nose-to-nose roll. And she felt as if she'd been given the world.

To make a wounded man smile?

No. She'd come here for the dog, she reminded herself. And for Alice.

But this week seemed to have changed things for Bryn, her sense of satisfaction was well justified, and she might even feel sad about leaving tomorrow.

Who was she kidding? *Might?* She knew she'd feel desolate. But she had to leave. Hazel had to return to Sydney. Maureen was holding the fort, but she could only work part-time and there was no one to run the clinic. Even if there was a point in her staying...well, why would she?

Bryn had been smiling as he watched kid and dog roll, but as he reached her his smile faded. He was still gazing down at them, but his face was suddenly grim.

'Problem?' she asked, and he took a deep breath and turned to face her.

'Kiara, I need you to stay.' Then, as she opened

her mouth to respond, he held up a hand. 'Please. Hear me out. This isn't for me—or for Alice. This is desperation.'

And briefly he outlined what he'd just been told.

'I know you think it's impossible,' he told her. 'But Sydney Central is without its three senior neurologists. There's no one else in the short term. Kiara, if I don't head back, people will die.'

What was he asking? She stared at him in open-mouthed astonishment. 'You're kidding.'

'I don't think I am,' he said bleakly. 'Archie's looked at every option. He's desperate. But I can't leave Alice. Kiara, I've tried to think but I can't get past it. There's no one but you.'

'So ring Beatrice,' she managed, feeling winded. More. She was feeling almost as if a gun were being pointed at her head. She had needs. Her dogs were her life.

'If I don't head back, people will die...'

The medical imperative. Unarguable.

'Do you think Beatrice would come?' he asked.

She stared at him for a long time, playing it out in her head. Thinking of what she knew of the acerbic Beatrice. 'No,' she said at last.

'Neither do I.'

And then they were silent because Alice and Bunji were at the top of the slope again. They watched as kid and dog repeated their roll, as they ended up in a tangle of arms, legs, tail at the bottom. As Bunji was cuddled. As Alice was licked. They were content, Kiara thought, and she thought of the miracle it had taken to get them this far.

'There's a child-minding service at the hospital,' Bryn said at last, talking heavily, as if the weight of the world were on his shoulders. As maybe it was. 'Archie's asked. It's for littlies, but because it's an emergency they'll take Alice until I can find someone else. But I can't bear...'

And neither could she. The thought of Alice being left in a strange setting...without Bunji...

'No,' she said, and Bryn raked his already rumpled hair.

'Kiara, I know I have no right to ask, but is there anyone else to take on Two Tails? I'm prepared to pay as much as Beatrice has already paid you. Per week. Just until Archie can find replacements, or until the new school term starts? You need cash and I need help. Could it work?'

He was serious?

She turned and looked down the slope, at Alice and Bunji, mutually engrossed in blowing dandelion seeds. How had a dandelion dared show its face in this perfectly manicured garden?

Who knew?

What was he asking?

That she step in and take over care of dog and child, so he could go back to his perfectly manicured life?

No. That was unfair. She'd read enough about the work he did to realise that his statement—*'people will die'*—was probably the truth.

'It's three weeks,' he said.

'Until boarding school?'

'I know that's no longer an option. Even I can see how much she needs Bunji. But I've been making enquiries. There's a local school only four blocks from here. It seems to have a good reputation. I've talked to the headmistress. There's only a week before end of term so we've agreed Alice can start in three weeks' time. But, Kiara, I don't have three weeks. I've wasted enough time.'

Whoa…

I've wasted enough time?

All at once she was thinking back to the time after she'd been bitten by the snake. Danger over, both her grandmother and her father were at her hospital bedside, discussing her convalescence.

Her grandmother had been due to leave on a visit to a beloved sister in Perth. She'd laid her plans long since. Her flights had been booked for a year.

But her father had stood there, arms folded,

angry, unmoving. 'You'll have to take her,' he'd snapped. 'I've wasted enough time.'

Her grandmother had taken her—of course she had, and it had only been much later that Kiara had realised how much of a sacrifice missing that trip had been. But she'd known enough to accept without question that she had a place in her grandma's heart.

And here was another man, his face set, demanding someone else accept his responsibilities. Knowing that his life was far more important.

'I've wasted enough time.'

She opened her mouth to snap—but then she paused.

He'd closed his eyes and when he opened them again what she saw was a weariness that was almost bone deep. Months of shock, of pain and a responsibility he'd never asked for had left their indelible mark.

'Sorry, that was badly said,' he said at last. 'I haven't wasted my time. Believe it or not, I do care. I'm doing my best, and this has come at me from left field. I know this feels like emotional blackmail but I'm desperate for help. Kiara, I need you.'

'But I can't,' she managed. She was feeling desperate herself. 'My friend Hazel has been looking after Two Tails and she has to leave. I have dogs in care. I have a vet clinic to run.

Like your hospital, there's no one else who has the skills and availability. If Hazel agrees to stay on at Two Tails, then she loses her job. If I don't go back to Two Tails, my dogs will starve.' She shook her head, thinking of the impossibility of what he was asking. 'And, Bryn, honestly, it's not fair to Alice to make her more dependent on me. It's you she needs to learn to love, not me. You and your friend Archie need to find a Plan B.'

'There's no Plan B.'

'Well, I'm not Plan A.'

She felt sick, but what choice did she have? The thought of abandoning Two Tails… She couldn't do it. No!

And then, because any further discussion would achieve nothing, she crossed her arms across her chest, and she lay down on the grass.

'No,' she said again and rolled deliberately away down the slope.

Plan B. What the hell was Plan B?

And why, when there were so many convoluted problems filling his head, did he suddenly want to forget them all and roll down after her? Kiara had obviously managed to put away her anger. Woman and child and dog were now in a tangle of licks and laughter below.

Joining them would be more than stupid. He'd

end up twisting his mending knee, setting himself back months.

He needed to block out emotion—block out desire?—and think.

Kiara's refusal was understandable. It wasn't fair to demand it of her, but for the life of him he couldn't think of an alternative.

It was three weeks before Alice could start school. The thought of Alice in hospital childcare… He couldn't do it. If he offered more—a lot more—to an employment agency he might well find someone willing to work for him, but employing a stranger, expecting her to care for Alice full-time and hoping Alice didn't retreat again into her shell… Once again, he couldn't do it.

He had two conflicting imperatives, and they *were* imperative. He had to start work, but he was Alice's guardian. He had to do what was best for her.

And it wasn't just that he was her guardian, he thought as he watched the group below him. With Kiara's help he'd grown closer to Alice this week than he'd been since she'd arrived. If he could wave his wand and send her back to the States he wouldn't do it, not unless he was convinced it'd make her happier. Boarding school was out of the question. Like it or not, she was now part of his life, living here with him, for… how long?

For however long she needed.

And that brought back what Kiara said. That Alice needed to learn to love him.

That thought was practically overwhelming, and he shoved it away with force. One day at a time, he told himself, fighting back panic.

And suddenly, through the panic, there was Plan B.

He checked it out, examining it from all angles and finding it…okay.

Three weeks. Trust was already established. It might even be good for all of them.

'Kiara,' he called.

She looked up, wary. He should head down the slope and join them, but rolling was out of the question and his leg was too stiff to try walking. He'd have to use the path, which would look wussy.

Besides, by the time he reached them they might well have climbed back up again.

Not for the first time he cursed his injured leg. Not only had Skye's death blindsided him emotionally, he was accustomed to his body doing what he demanded. Now…these last months had left him feeling as if he were on quicksand. He longed, no, even stronger, he *yearned* to be back at work. Back where emotional and physical injuries were his to treat, not his to endure.

Cutting-edge medicine had always been his retreat from emotion. The hospital needed him and suddenly, more than ever, he longed for it as well. The emotions he was feeling were starting to seem overwhelming.

'Kiara,' he called, louder, and she looked doubtfully up at him, said something to Alice he couldn't hear and then made her way back up the slope. Then she stood, hands behind her back. Dutiful employee waiting for orders?

Employee until tomorrow?

'I've had a thought,' he said.

'That's great.' She nodded encouragingly. 'Thoughts are good.' He glowered, and infuriatingly she tried a smile—trying to make light of an impossible situation? 'As long as it doesn't involve me abandoning my responsibilities, I'm all ears,' she told him. 'Tell me your thought.'

She was teasing?

She was like an annoying buzz fly, he thought. Deserving of swatting.

Honestly?

Honestly, despite the pressure he was under, right at this minute he didn't want to swat her.

Of all the inappropriate thoughts he could have, he actually, stupidly, wanted to kiss her.

He was so far out of his comfort zone here. He

needed to pull himself together. He was in a mess enough. A kiss…even if he didn't get slapped, it'd make what he was about to suggest a whole lot more complicated.

So get on with it, he told himself fiercely. Outline Plan B.

'What if you take Alice and Bunji to your place?'

'Pardon?' She looked at him blankly.

'I'd pay you to keep them at this refuge of yours,' he said, quickly, sensing her first instinct would be to reject it out of hand. 'Kiara, Alice likes you a lot. She's old enough to be little trouble, and Bunji would be safe. I could pay you to care for them for the three weeks until Alice starts school.'

'Really?' she said slowly. 'And then what?'

'By then I'll have sorted the mess at work. Sydney Central has a great reputation—we'll find new people. My pressure will ease, and Alice can come home again.'

'Define home.'

He frowned. 'Where she lives, of course.'

'So you agree that she lives here?'

'It doesn't stop her being somewhere else for a while. She can't depend on me for everything.'

And at that he copped it again, a flash of anger from her dark eyes.

'So who can she depend on?'

'I meant—'

'I know exactly what you meant,' she told him. 'Alice can depend on you in an emergency—like when her mother dies, or when you have time and space to allow her to share your life. But as for being there whenever—'

'I can't put my life on hold.'

'For a child. Why not? What bigger reason is there? I told you. What Alice needs is someone to love her, and that someone can't be me.'

She paused then and took a few deep breaths. She turned away and looked down the slope again, obviously thinking, and when she finally turned back, she had her face under control. The anger was gone, but when she spoke again her voice was flat. Decisive.

'Okay,' she said. 'If it really is life or death that the hospital gets its precious neurosurgeon—and, yes, I believe you—then for Alice's sake I'll let her come with me. But on one condition.'

'What's that?'

'That you come, too.'

'But—'

'No buts. That's my offer and you can take it or leave it. For whatever you think, Alice needs a home in the true sense of the word. She's the same as Bunji. Bunji seems to have found her home with Alice, but Alice's home needs to be you. Not me. You. So, Dr Dalton, it's up to you.

You can come and go to work as you please—go save the world—but every night you need to come home to Alice. I'll provide three weeks' board and lodging, care and kindness to Alice and Bunji while you're away, but for these three weeks, Alice's home is still you. As it has to be, now and for ever. So…deal?'

Three weeks…

Now and for ever?

What was she asking?

But he looked down into her face and what he saw there was implacable. Take it or leave it.

Three weeks away from his home.

Home? She was saying it had a whole new definition.

He couldn't process it, but he was up against a brick wall, and he knew it.

Could it hurt to spend three weeks in this refuge he'd only heard about?

'Is it big enough?'

'I have four bedrooms,' she told him. 'Two of them are habitable and I have an attic I think Alice might love.' She glanced around at his swimming pool, his manicured lawns, his stunning house. 'It's not quite up to your standard,' she confessed. 'But if you're prepared to slum it…'

'Slum it…'

'Well, maybe not slum exactly. Two Tails might

be wonky but it's clean, and it is a home. So, what do you think, Dr Dalton? Last offer?'

He stared at her, and she gazed back, her look direct and challenging.

Okay, he thought. It'd take longer but he could travel to work from her place. It might even do Alice good.

But then... Three more weeks staying with this woman?

What was there in that that gave him pause?

Pause or not, he had no choice.

'Thank you,' he said weakly.

'You're welcome,' she told him, and she smiled a tight smile, then turned away and proceeded to roll down the slope again.

CHAPTER EIGHT

WHAT HAD HE EXPECTED?

Given the state of Kiara's finances, some sort of dog pens, and a run-down house attached?

It might be run-down, but it was beautiful.

He'd followed Kiara in her battered van as she'd driven back to Two Tails, and when she pulled into the drive, he could only stare.

The house was built at the beginning of a valley, the road in front winding on to the town of Birralong. From here the land was zoned a national park, thick, untouched bushland, fantastical gorges, a landscape as wild as it was beautiful.

The house itself was a cottage, weathered with age but stunningly beautiful. A wilderness of garden was practically taking over. Crimson bougainvillea washed across the corrugated roof and trailed along the wide veranda. Huge eucalypts formed a vast, bird-filled backdrop, and the peaks of the Blue Mountains towered in the distance.

A discreet sign on the front door said *Two Tails. Please Ring and Wait.* Another sign said *Clinic* and pointed to a winding path leading to the left.

'Wow!' Alice had driven with Kiara, and now she and Bunji were out of Kiara's battered van. The little girl was looking as awed as he felt. 'This is where you live?' she asked Kiara.

'It's my home,' Kiara told her, and the way she said it told him how much she loved it.

This was why she'd given them Bunji, he reminded himself. And it was why they were here now. This was a paid service.

The door opened and an elderly woman with a mass of wild, white curls appeared in the doorway. 'Oh, Kiara. Thank heaven you're back. Hazel had to go in a hurry, so I stayed on, but my Jim's got a doctor's appointment. So this is Alice. And you must be Dr Dalton. Pleased to meet you, I'm sure. Kiara, sorry, love, but I need to be off.' And she grabbed a battered purse from inside the hall and bolted.

'That's Maureen,' Kiara told Alice. 'She tries to do way too much, but she's awesome. She was my grandma's best friend. She treats me as if I'm a kid, and she'll treat you just the same. She's bossy but she's great.' She hesitated and then added: 'Sometimes I think without Maureen I might fall apart. But come on in. Alice, Maureen's set up a room I think you'll love. It's in the attic and it's very private, your own personal space. The stairs up are a bit wonky, but it has a great gable window looking out to the mountains. I asked Maureen to put some of my favourite books in there, plus a pile of bedding for Bunji. Would you like to see?'

And Alice cast her a look of wonder and headed upstairs without a backward glance.

She'd turned into a child again, Bryn thought. What had happened to her in the last week?

Kiara had happened.

She was standing beside him, watching kid and dog bounce up the stairs. 'They have their brave back,' she said, smiling as they disappeared.

'Thanks to you.'

'I know, I'm a matchmaker,' she said smugly. 'Bunji and Alice—a match made in heaven.'

He looked at her curiously. There was so much he didn't understand about this woman. 'So how about you?' He had no business asking but he couldn't help himself. 'Have you made any matches for yourself?'

She cast him an odd look. 'You know, since I'm your employee I'm pretty sure you're not supposed to ask that question.' And then her irrepressible smile peeped out again. 'But no. I have nine dogs here and who has time—or the need—for a love life when there are nine dogs requiring as much love as I can give them? When they've all found their forever homes, there might be time for me.'

'But there'll always be dogs.'

'I guess there will,' she admitted. 'Even if I can no longer run Two Tails.' She spread her hand, encompassing the big living room they'd just entered. 'Maybe I'll just live in poverty here, letting the termites do their worst around me. I'll be a modern Ms Havisham, but with termites and dogs instead of cobwebs. There are surely worse places to be stuck.'

Maybe there were.

But…

The Miss Havisham reference—Dickens' fictional jilted bride, dwindling into old age in her decrepit house—could never be a reasonable comparison, he thought, but there were points of resemblance. He was gazing around with a certain amount of awe. How could one person have all this…stuff?

But it wasn't just 'stuff'. Fascinated, he started to prowl. How could one room contain so many pictures? Piles of bric-a-brac loaded each side table. The room was crowded with eclectic furniture, crazy lamps. What looked at first glance to be almost a product of hoarding was, on second, third, even fourth inspection, a massive collection of personal wonder.

'Did you gather all this?' he asked, stunned, and she gave a self-conscious laugh.

'Grandma was a bower bird. She loved history, loved the stories of her people, but she and her sister lost most of their family and I think she collected things to make up for it. Once she lost my mother, her collecting seemed to become even more frenetic.'

He lifted a wooden carving, a piece of ironbark magnificently formed into a figure of woman and child. 'This should be on public display.'

'I love it.'

'Of course.' He frowned. 'But all of this? You love it all?'

'You haven't seen the half of it,' she admitted. 'Every room is crammed. And, no, I don't love most of it—dusting it is a nightmare—but I have no idea what to do with it. If...when I leave here it'll have to be sold. Or donated. The local charity shop will be grateful.'

'Don't you dare.'

She flashed him a look of surprise. 'Because?'

'Because it's worth...' Once more he gazed around. One of the women he'd dated, a top of the trees' radiologist, had been a collector of old porcelain. For the few months they'd been together—a long time in the history of his brief relationships—he'd indulged her by spending weekends prowling junk shops and car boot sales. He knew the crazy prices people paid, and what Kiara had here was a goldmine. 'If you really want to get rid of it, it'll bring heaps,' he said at last, feeling the inadequacy of the word. 'I have friends who know the right people to value it, to help you sort it, so you get what it's worth.'

'Really?'

'Really. No pressure but I'm thinking Two Tails is just as deserving of cash as your local charity shop.'

She flushed and smiled, and then shook her head. 'I'm sure most of it's worthless.'

'And some of it isn't. This bowl…' He lifted a crimson and green glass bowl that was filled with potpourri and held it to the light. 'I know someone who'd pay serious money for this. Enough to keep even Bunji in dog food for a month.'

'Really? That much? Wow!' She smiled. For the last week Bunji had suddenly found her appetite, wolfing down each meal and pleading for more. But then she shrugged, moving on. 'It's a possibility,' she conceded. 'But you've helped me enough. I'll show you to your room.'

'Show me more,' he urged. 'Where do you keep your dogs?'

She cast him a doubtful glance and then led the way out to the back of the house. Here the veranda morphed into a line of dog pens, each a small 'cubby' under the extended roofline of the veranda. The enclosures opened at the rear, so each dog had its individual run. The runs were wide and generous, running down to the lawn and ending under the shade of the eucalypts.

The pens seemed to be three quarters empty. 'We're whittling down,' Kiara told him, seeing his enquiring look. 'Bunji was the last dog we took. We have tentative homes for most of these but they're undertaking training before they go. We don't just rehouse, we rehome. See Mickey, the corgi? He's eight years old, a gentle lamb, but his owner died two months ago. He's being retrained for Shirley, who's in her seventies and has rheumatoid arthritis. She lives in a second-floor apartment, so we're training him to use a doggy door through to the fire escape, which leads to a little backyard. He's had two sessions so far. Hazel says the last time he was brilliant. I thought Alice might like to come with me this week while I take him for one last trial. Then he's set to go.'

She headed over to let Mickey out, stooping to scratch behind his ears. 'You know, Bunji's pretty clever,' she said thoughtfully. 'She might even help.'

'You're a trained vet,' he said, cautiously. 'You spend your time teaching dogs to use fire escapes?'

'Hey, I do lots of vet stuff, too,' she retorted. 'I run a clinic for a couple of hours every afternoon. But rehoming successfully is what I love.'

'And when you leave here?'

Her brightness faded. 'I guess… If I have to leave then I'll just go back to being a normal vet. Patching up and moving on.'

Well, maybe that was no bad fate, he decided, as she led him through the pens and introduced him to her weird mix of clients. That was what *he* did, after all. He patched people up and moved on.

No emotional attachment there.

'So,' she said briskly. 'Let's get you settled and then you can head off to work as you will. As long as you're home at a reasonable hour for Alice, then I'm happy to keep her entertained. All these guys are pretty much certified bombproof. My grounds are dog safe. Apart from the fussy ones who think romping in a paddock is beneath them, Alice can walk as many as she wants. I have a feeling she'll like that, and so will my dogs.' She hesitated. 'She's a loner—she's had to be. Hopefully you'll break that down, but she'll still need space.'

'I guess.' He thought of the psychology sessions he'd organised for Alice and thought…this woman is helping just as much, if not more.

'I have clinic at three,' she was saying, oblivious to where his thoughts were taking him. 'But I'm still just through that door if Alice needs me, and it shouldn't take long. I've put notices in the local paper saying clients need to start thinking of where they'll go when we close, and we've already noticed a drop off.'

'You'll miss this place.'

'Like a hole in my heart,' she admitted, her voice tightening. 'But as you—and especially Alice—already know, holes just have to be papered over if you're to move on.'

He was back! Gloriously he was back in his rooms at Sydney Central. His receptionist, assigned to other duties while he was away, had returned to her rightful desk. Apart from her concerned question… 'Do I need to space appointments, give you time to adjust?'…she was acting as if he'd simply been overseas to a conference.

He fielded a few concerned queries about his leg from his colleagues. There were brief quips about idiots who didn't leave rescues to those who knew how, but then the ripples caused by his absence simply moved to the horizon and disappeared. The gossip about Rod and Caroline had overtaken almost everything, and their absence caused pressure on the whole department.

Was that why there was no talk of Alice? No one asked. Or was it that the advent of a child in his life wasn't supposed to affect him at all?

But this was what he'd longed for—demanding, technical work that necessarily blocked out all the emotion of the last few months. Work, where he could be self-contained, fully focused on the highly skilled procedures that saved people's lives. Work, where he didn't need to think about Alice and her needs.

Where he didn't have to think about Kiara?

How had Kiara come into the equation? He had no clue, but both Alice and Kiara stayed in his mind.

He'd always had the ability to focus solely on what was at hand. This subconscious backdrop of Alice—and Kiara—was disturbing.

His first hour or so, of necessity, had to be spent at his desk, catching up on what had to be done, on the mess that had been left by his two colleagues. It was Saturday. There'd hopefully be no urgent surgery today, but Archie and Rebecca had moved some of Rod's urgent consults to this afternoon. He thus had to be totally focused, and he was fast immersed in patient histories, consulting with radiologists over results from MRIs, consideration of medications, alternatives to surgery. Discussion of dangers, for and against. Assessments of possible outcomes of surgery.

He had to be at the top of his game, and part of him welcomed it—this had been what he'd ached for over the last months.

But still, part of him was separate. Part of his mind was back at home with Kiara.

No. Home with Alice, he reminded himself harshly, and then he thought… Home?

Wasn't home back in Clovelly?

But maybe his real home was here, at the beating hub of a huge teaching hospital. Here, where he'd felt more in control of his world than in any other place, ever.

Except now he didn't. He felt…

As if he needed to give himself a decent shake and get on with it?

He had no choice. A family was ushered in, a kid with epilepsy. He'd made a thorough study of his history before he saw him, previous treatments and prognosis. He was tentatively scheduled to do the surgery Rod had recommended, and now he had to say it as it was.

'With this procedure there's over a fifty per cent chance that your epilepsy will subside to the point where it can be well controlled by medication.' Felix was fifteen years old, a kid whose epilepsy was spiralling out of control. His parents were sitting behind him, having the sense to let their son do the talking. Letting Felix make the calls. Even so, they were clutching each other's hands as if they were drowning.

'I just want to get better,' Felix muttered, and his mother couldn't contain herself any longer.

'But not if it's dangerous.'

This surgery came with risks—he outlined them, and they hung over the little group. There was a fifty per cent chance of massive improvement, maybe a thirty per cent chance of some improvement, but there was still a possibility of no improvement at all. Also...he had to admit that there was a minute risk of death.

He watched the parents blench, but not the kid, and who could blame him? 'I want to be able to kick a footy without everyone making a huge fuss,' he muttered. 'Like I am, they won't let me on the team. And as soon as I'm eighteen I want to drive a car. I want to be normal.'

'What would you do if it was your son?' his mother quavered, and her husband interjected.

'Yeah, Doc. If it was your family...your kid... If it was your wife you'd have to hold up if things go pear-shaped...'

And there they were again, front and centre. Kiara and Alice.

Kiara.

He thought of her perky grin, her spirit. He

thought of Kiara with her arms folded, rolling down the slope to join Bunji and Alice.

He thought of her, head bent over Bunji's healing wound, skilfully debriding but speaking to the dog in such soothing tones she hardly needed anaesthetic.

He thought of Kiara, organising Alice her attic room, acknowledging that Alice still needed space to be alone.

He just thought…of Kiara.

'It'd probably be my wife who'd do the holding up,' he said at last, because the group was waiting for an answer. If it could help this group by inferring he had a wife…if it'd help a decision…

For whatever reason, the sudden image of Kiara as his family helped him form his response.

'I guess, whatever happens, you hold each other up,' he said. 'Because that's what families do.'

That was what Kiara would do.

Enough. He needed to stop thinking about Kiara and move on without her in his head. He turned back to Felix. 'But you know what? If you're prepared to go through a few tough weeks after surgery, then there should be no holding up to be done at all. You won't need it.'

As he didn't need holding up?

Of course he didn't. It was only Alice…

'We'll always need it,' Felix's father said soundly. 'Doc, I side-swiped my brand-new car against the garage wall this morning. Inattention. Worrying about this appointment. But you know what? It was Felix who hugged me. Who held me up. We're a family, mate. Whatever the outcome there'll always be holding up to be done, and no matter what Felix decides, we're in this together.'

And there it was, decision made. Bryn sent them back to Rebecca to organise dates, times, pre-admission forms, and he moved on. Still feeling unsettled.

Two more patients and he could head home.

Home. There was that word again.

He worked on, and then, just as he was packing to leave, the call came in from the emergency department.

'Are you up for some tricky surgery, mate?' the head of ER asked him. 'We know you're only just back, but we're coping with a multiple-car pile-up, major trauma. We have a young guy with a skull fracture, a major cerebral bleed. Can you deal?'

There was no choice. For the first time ever, though, there were consequences for him. Kiara's words replayed. *'As long as you're home at a reasonable hour for Alice...'* He phoned Kiara and told her what had happened.

'The kid's seventeen,' he said. 'I need...'

'Of course you need,' she told him, and then spoke to Alice in the background. 'Hey, Alice, a kid's been in a car crash and the hospital wants your uncle to sew him up. Can we cope without him, or should we let our pizza get cold while we pine for him?'

'What's pine?' he heard Alice ask.

'It means sit on the back doorstep and cry because he's late and we miss him so much. What's it to be, Alice? We eat crunchy pizza without your uncle, or we cry into soggy tissues while we wait for him?'

And to his astonishment he heard a giggle. 'Pizza,' Alice decreed, and Kiara chuckled as well.

'Good choice. You heard that, Dr Dalton? You get on with saving lives and we promise we'll leave at least two slices of pizza in the microwave for you.'

He disconnected and headed for Theatre, but, stupidly, now part of him…part of him ached to be home.

Home.

To microwaved pizza.

To his…family?

CHAPTER NINE

IT WAS AFTER nine before he arrived back at Two Tails. The surgery had been a success. He should be pleased with himself, but instead he was as drained as he'd ever felt.

Three months away from work, a full day moving around, followed by four hours in Theatre had tested his gammy leg to the limits. And driving home…for some reason the emotions he'd felt as he'd talked to Felix came flooding back. Was he going home to family? He had little idea of the concept, but it surely didn't apply to coming home to Two Tails.

Coming home to wife and child and dog? The thought was…unnerving. He was far too tired to think about processing it.

The front door was unlocked. He knocked but when he received no answer he went on in.

Kiara and Alice and Benji were all in the living room. The vast open fire formed a soft glow behind them. Kiara was sitting on a rug before the fire, reading.

Alice was lying beside her, her head on Kiara's knee. A fluffy rug was wrapped around her. Asleep?

Bunji was lying full length beside them both. She opened her eyes as Bryn entered, offered a lazy wag of her tail and then went back to the important job of snoozing.

He stopped dead. It was such a picture. For Alice to be this relaxed, to be sleeping on Kiara's knee… Kiara's hand was on her wispy hair, gently stroking.

She looked up as Bryn entered, laid down her book and put a finger to her lips. 'Shh…'

He came and sat beside them—on the settee because it seemed far too familiar to sit on the rug itself.

'Welcome home,' Kiara whispered, and what was there in that to make his gut twist? 'How did it go?'

'One seventeen-year-old who'll live to do something stupid again, I dare say,' he told her. 'Joyriding. Kids.'

'But you succeeded.'

'Impossible to say for sure until he wakes up but I'm hopeful. We got the pressure off fast.'

'Well done, you,' she said and smiled and there was that gut twist again. 'So, pizza… It won't be great but it's edible. If you're anything like me, you can subsist quite nicely on reheated dinners.'

'Too many wounded dogs in your life?'

'And too many wounded kids in yours,' she said gently. But then Alice stirred a little and she hesitated. 'Actually… Bryn, are you up to helping her up to bed?'

He frowned. 'She didn't want to go herself?'

'She was waiting for you. She was trying to stay awake, but it's been too big a day. It'd be great for her to have you tuck her into bed.'

'Kiara…'

'Mmm?' The look she gave him was of innocent enquiry, but he had her figured by now. Ever since he'd met her, every step of the way, she'd hauled him into Alice's life.

Why did it make him feel he needed to back away?

But still he stooped and lifted Alice—she was such a featherweight that with the help of the bannisters he could even do it with his gammy leg. And when she woke and questioned him, he told her yes, he'd managed to sew the kid from the car accident up, and yes, he'd have a scar but he'd be okay.

'Like Bunji,' Alice murmured as he carried her upstairs, and then added sleepily… 'Like me.'

'Like all of us,' he said, tucking her into bed and then, because it seemed like the right thing to do, even though she'd shied from any sort of affectionate gesture from the time he'd met her, he bent and kissed her on the forehead. And to his amazement her skinny arms clung and hugged.

'I'm glad you're home,' she whispered. 'Is Bunji here?'

Bunji had followed them up the stairs and was indeed now in the bundle of rugs beside the bed.

He took Alice's hand and guided it down to lie on Bunji's soft head, and then he left them to sleep. And as he made his way down the stairs, he was suddenly overcome with a stupid urge to weep.

For heaven's sake…he must be more tired than he thought. He gave himself a moment at the foot of the stairs to recover, and then headed back into the living room.

Kiara had cleared the muddle on the coffee table to make room for a plate of pizza and a glass of wine. She was on the rug again. She was wearing shabby jeans and a faded windcheater. Her dusky curls were loose and tousled, her shabby windcheater was way too big for her…and he thought he'd never seen anyone as beautiful.

He needed to pull himself together.

'Dinner,' she said, and he sank down onto the

armchair and looked at what was before him. And looked again.

Yes, it was pizza, but this was like no pizza he'd ever had delivered. A thick, buttery crust. Tiny baked tomatoes. Fresh…*everything.* Vegetables that had obviously been grilled beforehand—tiny mushrooms, red peppers, aubergine, zucchini… He could smell herbs…oregano? Thyme? Gorgonzola cheese had been sliced and spread to melt as the pizza cooked, then black pepper sprinkled on and finally a scattering of fresh basil.

'This is leftover pizza?' he said, stunned.

'Pizza's one of my splinter skills,' she said proudly. 'Yours isn't quite up to scratch because of the reheating, but I have a microwave with a pizza function. It's therefore not as soggy as it might have been.'

It looked fine to him. More, it looked great. 'I thought you said you didn't cook.'

'I cook pizza.'

'You made the whole thing?' For heaven's sake, he sounded accusatory.

'I make a heap of dough and freeze individual servings,' she told him. 'So yes, Alice and I made it, but we didn't make it from scratch. Without my store of frozen bases, I'd never have tried them at your place. And,' she added smugly, 'apart from the cheese, the topping's all from my veggie patch. Except for the mushrooms, which are from my little mushroom factory in the back of the hall cupboard. And there's another lack in your fancy house. I checked your hall cupboard and found not a single mushroom.'

He had to smile back. As far as he knew, his hall cupboard contained one winter coat and one squash racket. It was dusted and aired regularly by his housekeepers. No mushroom would dare show its face.

'Did Alice eat hers?'

'Yes, she did.' She still had that smug smile, and, wow, her smile was infectious. 'Hers might not have looked quite like ours, though,' she confessed. 'She made her own, with tomato sauce, cheese and bacon, and we used a bone-shaped cookie cutter to make her base into mini pizzas. I occasionally make doggy biscuits for my clients. We had to sterilise my cookie cutter to make sure it was an okay for pizzas, but her bone-shape pizzas were excellent.'

He thought of Alice, of how little she'd eaten over the last weeks. Alice, eating bone-shaped pizzas. 'You're a marvel.'

'I know,' she said smugly. 'Now, if you'll excuse me, I'm up to a very exciting part of my book.'

And that was that. She tucked Alice's rug

around her knees and disappeared into her story. Leaving him to enjoy his dinner.

Which was, in itself, extraordinary.

He thought briefly back through the long list of women he'd dated over the years. Of nights spent. Not one of them would abandon talking to disappear into a book.

But this wasn't dating.

No. It was more than that. It felt…comfortable. He'd come home stressed and tired, fighting emotions he was struggling to understand. He was aware that he was late, aware that there were responsibilities facing him. And instead of more stress, he'd carried a sleeping child up to her bedroom and been hugged. He'd been handed a truly excellent meal, with wine. He'd been allowed to sink into a saggy armchair by an open fire and just…be.

The sensation was extraordinary.

She was sitting beside him, leaning back on an armchair, knees tucked up, rug tucked over her. She was frowning with intent at something she was reading.

There was a wisp of a curl dangling down over her forehead. Close to blocking her sight. It needed to be brushed back.

She was too intent on her story.

Dammit, he couldn't help himself. He leaned

forward and wove his finger through the curl, tucking it behind her ear.

She looked up at him, surprised, but not alarmed. It had been an intensely personal gesture, but she didn't seem to have noticed.

'Thanks,' she said and smiled up at him—and went straight back into her book.

He was left with his pizza and his wine.

He was left feeling…winded.

And that was how their days went. One following another.

He left every morning for Sydney Central, Alice and Kiara waving him off as if this were part of a lifetime routine.

He couldn't believe how quickly Alice had settled. She was practically blooming. Bunji was hardly limping now, her fur was growing almost to the point where she looked respectable, and she followed Alice with slave-like devotion. Kid and dog were happy.

Kiara was busy. Maureen usually arrived before Bryn left for work and settled into whatever needed doing. She and Alice seemed to become immediate friends, but she could usually only fit in two or three hours. Kiara therefore had little help. Each of the dogs had a training routine, she had clinic to run, but somehow, she seamlessly wove Alice and Bunji into her day. By the time he left for work they were out in the paddock, teaching dogs to heel, to recall, not to jump up when excited.

And every morning when he left, he was aware of a pang of loss. He wouldn't mind being out there with them.

Which was stupid. His career was medicine. His *life* was medicine. Kiara was simply taking over part of his responsibility for Alice, while he returned to where he belonged. At the end of the term break, Alice would start at her new school. They'd be back at Clovelly. They'd be back at their new normal.

With Rebecca's help he'd hired a housekeeper from another agency—a woman he interviewed in a brief break from work, a week after they'd been at Two Tails. Mrs Connor seemed pleasant, happy with the prospect of taking on the care of Alice and Bunji. 'I have dogs of my own and I'm a grandma,' she told him. 'My husband's retired and my sister lives with us, so I won't need to rush if you get stuck at work.'

She seemed excellent. His future was therefore starting to feel in control again.

Except...where was Kiara in this picture?

Nowhere, and nor should she be. She'd been employed to do a job. She was doing it handsomely and she'd be paid. Then they'd move on.

With a bit of luck, she might agree to keeping

in touch with Alice, he thought, and he told himself that was all there was to it. But as the days passed, the more he thought that wasn't enough. The relationship between woman and child…it was like gold.

And then there was…the way he felt.

If he got back to Two Tails early enough, he'd usually find them in the kitchen. 'I don't usually cook when there's just me,' Kiara told him when he queried it. 'But Alice and I are pulling out Grandma's recipe books and having fun.'

If he came home later, he'd find them curled up before the fire with books that Kiara had found from her childhood. Alice would be entranced, while Bunji snoozed beside them. He'd carry Alice to bed and be hugged goodnight and then return to the fireside.

To Kiara.

More and more the word family was messing with his thoughts.

'How do you know how to make Alice so happy?' Alice was now in bed, he was on his second glass of wine, his leg had miraculously stopped aching and he felt…okay.

'I guess… Grandma,' she said simply. 'Grandma never treated me as a kid—or if she did it was only when she was acting like a kid herself. Anything I know about happiness I learned from Grandma.'

They were in their customary positions, he in his favourite squashy chair, she on the rug, her book ready to be sunk back into. She loved thrillers, she'd told him. The darker the better, and he'd started watching her face as she read, watching her eyes grow rounder as the story got gorier.

He loved watching her.

That errant curl had dropped again. He badly wanted to tuck it back again.

He didn't dare. If he let himself touch her…

'So how about you?' she asked as he fought back the urge to move closer. 'I've told you about me, so tit for tat. Three siblings who don't seem to know each other. What's the story there?'

'Money.'

'Money?' She appeared to think about it. 'I guess,' she said at last. 'I hear it does weird things to families. I wouldn't mind getting involved in some sort of social research myself. If someone were to offer me, say, a million dollars, to see how much it messes with my life, maybe I'd even take the risk.' She ventured a cautious smile. 'But go on. Don't mind me. Tell me the appalling things that money did.'

And he had to smile back. She was irrepressible.

She was gorgeous.

She was waiting for his story—which wasn't nearly as gorgeous.

Nor was it as bad as hers.

'Just…socialite stuff,' he told her. 'My father married three times. He probably would have added to the tally, but he died of a heart attack when I was eighteen. Before that, he was the heir to serious money, and he was pretty much a serial womaniser. Beatrice was the result of his first marriage. Thea, his first wife, was related to royalty and stood no nonsense. She caught Dad having an affair with an American actress when Beatrice was two, and she took Beatrice straight back to England. Beatrice has been knee-deep in dogs and horses ever since. Dad then married his actress and they had Skye. I believe both of them had affairs, but that marriage ended for good when Skye was five, probably because Dad was having a very public affair with my mother. Mum had money and social connections and the affair hit the media. Thus his next marriage, and me, but that was also a disaster. Mum…just enjoyed the limelight. Domesticity wasn't her thing, and even now I scarcely know her. She walked out and married someone with even more money when I was three, but she didn't take me with her. So I was the only one left with Dad.'

'Ouch.'

'Not really ouch. I was well treated, big houses,

servants, nannies to cater for my every whim…' He tried to say it lightly, but it didn't come off.

'So no Grandma.'

'I do have a grandma somewhere,' he told her. 'On my mother's side. She's never shown the slightest interest in meeting me, and vice versa. I don't need family.'

'Everyone needs family.'

'You've managed okay.'

'I had Grandma until four years ago, and I have substitutes. My best friend Hazel—she's the one who found Bunji—she's always here for me. And Maureen… You only see her as a part-time worker, but she was my grandma's best friend and she'd lose an arm for me. Then there's this community…'

'Which you'll leave if you sell.'

Her face clouded. 'Yes,' she said shortly. 'But Two Tails was a dream, and maybe it's time to move on from dreams. Maybe I'll set up another such shelter in the future, when I've saved up again. Find another community somewhere a bit…'

'Cheaper?'

'I guess termite-ridden heritage cottages don't exactly fit my budget.' She gazed around the room, her eyes suddenly thoughtful. 'But not yet. What you're paying me will keep me afloat for a while and this Saturday…well, this is your idea, but Maureen and I have organised a yard sale.'

'A yard sale…'

'Yep.' She motioned to boxes he hadn't noticed at the side of the room. 'I'm not being dumb,' she told him. 'I rehoused an ancient Peke a while back with a gorgeous old lady—Maire. Her son, Howard, is incredibly grateful—and he runs a chain of antique shops. I asked him to come out and go through this place. If you look, he's now put stickers under everything he thinks would sell better at auction—or in one of his shops—and the rest will go in the yard sale. Donna, the local newsagent—she owns one of my greyhounds—has organised posters, plus social media stuff. Some of my clients are coming to help—they're adding cake stalls, fancy goods, you name it. There'll be balloons on the gate at seven a.m. Maureen and Alice and I are beyond excited.'

'You're selling a lot?' he said faintly, and here came that smile again.

'I am. Thanks to you. I don't know how it is but after Grandma died…well, the place was just…how it is. When you showed interest, I thought why am I keeping it? Grandma would love if it keeps Two Tails going a bit longer.'

'Kiara, let me help,' he said, suddenly sure. 'Financially. You know money's not an issue with me. I hate to think of you selling your belongings to keep it going. Maybe I could even become a silent partner. Whatever you need.'

What followed was a long silence. He could see her running the idea through her head as she considered it from all angles.

'Wow, that's a great offer,' she said at last, and she sounded a bit confused. Cautious. 'And part of me says yay. But there's another part… Bryn, that's hugely generous but I don't… I don't think I can do it.'

'Can I ask why not?'

'Because I'm stupid?'

'I'm very sure that's not the case.' He was watching an inward struggle, not sure where it was going.

'I guess…' She frowned. 'Look, it doesn't make sense, and maybe I should take time to consider, but my gut reaction… Bryn, it's that I don't want to be bought.'

'I'm not buying you.'

'No, but it's my life. I can't even explain. Only that Two Tails has been my dream, mine and Hazel's, and it's all done on our terms.'

'I wouldn't interfere.'

'No,' she said, doubtfully. 'But…' She hesitated again. 'Let me give you an example. Bunji. She came to me a mess, she's cost me a fortune and she was a huge risk. There was a strong probability that she'd either die or be unable to be rehomed. But the risk was mine.'

'I'd never interfere…'

'You wouldn't have to. You'd just be…there.' Once again, that hesitation, and he could see her struggle to find words. 'Bryn, it's Dad. He comes into play here. Whatever I wanted in life, he had control. When I finally got free, the feeling was amazing, and I never want to go back.'

'I'd never control.'

'You wouldn't have to. You'd just be there.'

'You wouldn't trust me?'

'You can't just turn on trust,' she said sadly. 'Look, I know it doesn't make sense, but I need to do this my way. I've accepted your salary and Beatrice's contribution with gratitude—it really will make a difference. I've run with your idea of selling some of Grandma's possessions and that'll make a difference, too. But, Bryn, I'm independent and you have no idea how important that is to me.'

'More important than keeping Two Tails running?' He heard a current of anger in his voice and had to bite it back.

Why was he angry? That she wouldn't allow him to help?

That she wouldn't allow him to be a part of her life going forward?

And maybe that was what she was afraid of.

He thought it and accepted it, and the anger died. If it was his independence that was being threatened, then maybe he'd feel the same way.

He *would* feel the same way.

So, he understood—or he thought he did. And he also understood the slight constraint as she picked up her book, rose and said goodnight.

'It's an incredible offer,' she said. 'I'm a fool not to accept and I know it. I don't even fully understand myself why I can't, but all I know is that it's the way things are for me.'

He rose, too. For a long moment she just looked at him, questioning? He wasn't sure why, but he had a strange feeling she was seeing something that maybe he didn't even understand himself. For suddenly she took a step forward, stood on tiptoes and kissed him. It was the same gesture she'd used before. Their lips brushed, for the most fleeting of moments, and it was done.

'I suspect we're two of a kind,' she said, and there was sadness in her voice now. 'Tarred with the same brush? So, I'm rejecting your offer for no reason at all, other than I don't know any other way to live. Thank you, Bryn, and goodnight.'

She'd just rejected an offer to keep Two Tails running. To keep her dream alive.

Why?

Because…of the way Bryn made her feel?

It was crazy and she couldn't explain it. But as she lay in the dark, searching for elusive sleep, she knew her explanation to Bryn wasn't the best she could do.

There was another underlying reason that was scaring her witless. The way she was starting to feel.

Of being out of control?

There was that word again. When she'd managed to escape her father's iron discipline, she'd vowed never to let herself be controlled again, but what Bryn was offering… Surely there was some way they could set things up…a financial partnership where she could still do as she willed… No control on his part at all?

He wouldn't interfere with her decisions to save her dogs. She knew him well enough to believe that.

But there was the problem. She knew him well enough, and part of her was starting to ache to know him better. Part of her felt that when he came home at night…no, when he came back to Two Tails, not home…that part of her was… complete. His smile as he walked through the door. His stoop to hug his little niece. His hug that embraced Bunji.

The way he smiled at her—and, oh, that smile…

It was nonsense, this way she was feeling, and

it had to stop. It made her feel as if her world were teetering and she didn't know what was on the downside of a fall.

It made her feel as if her precious control of her life was growing more and more fragile and she had to haul it back. To continue seeing him… to have him part of her life, even if it was only financially… It was starting to scare her. She was beginning to feel like a moonstruck teenager, and she had to pull back.

For some reason, letting Bryn Dalton any further into her life was a step that terrified her too much to contemplate.

CHAPTER TEN

SATURDAY. THE DAY of the yard sale.

There'd been an emergency at Sydney Central the night before. An aneurism, a young mum. Bryn had arrived home in the small hours, mentally and physically wiped. He'd expected the house to be in darkness, but Kiara must have heard his car pull into the yard as she'd come into the hall to greet him.

'How?' she'd asked simply, and he'd managed a tired smile. His leg was aching, he was exhausted, but underneath there was a tinge of hopeful triumph.

'We think she'll make it. She'll be in an induced coma for a few days to let the swelling subside, but the worst of the pressure's off. We can hope.'

'Well done, you,' she'd said, and for a moment he'd thought she might walk forward and hug him. And he badly wanted her to.

But neither of them had moved. 'If you want,

there's a bowl of pasta ready to be microwaved,' she'd said simply. 'Or toast and tea if you're past it.'

'Thank you.' He'd hesitated. 'I see the stalls are set up outside for the morning. Do you need help?'

'You sleep and let us worry about everything else,' she'd told him. 'Alice and I are into money making tomorrow. You need to recoup so you can keep on saving the world.' And once again there had been that moment of hesitation where he'd thought…hug?

It didn't happen. They were adults who knew where their boundaries lay.

'Goodnight,' she'd said simply, and disappeared back to her bedroom.

And he'd taken her at her word. He'd left his alarm off and slept, and it was almost nine when he woke. There was noise coming from the yard. He flipped back the curtains and saw…people. The yard was packed, and he could see a line of cars stretching back along the road until they were out of sight.

Ten minutes later he was outside, and Alice was racing to greet him, Bunji at her side.

'Bryn, come and see, come and see. Kiara gave me my own stall and it's all sold out. Grandma had shells—you must have seen them, she collected them for ever—and I sold the big ones for two dollars and the little ones for a dollar, and I've made a hundred and thirty-seven dollars! And Maureen made pink cupcakes, but she was feeling tired, so I helped her sell them, too. And the man called Howard is going to auction other stuff, and a whole lot of people have got dogs and they know who Bunji is, and there's even a dog-biscuit stall. Come and see!'

He couldn't believe it. His damaged, introverted niece, towing him around the yard as if she owned it.

It was a miracle. Kiara's miracle.

And here was Kiara, haggling with a gentleman over the sale of a hay-rake. She'd opened the run-down sheds at the back of the property to reveal her grandmother's mass of ancient farm equipment. There were prices on everything.

'It's vintage,' she was saying.

'It's a piece of junk. I could use it as scrap metal.'

'Howard says it's collectible and he also pointed you out as a dealer,' she said stoutly. 'He gave me a bottom price. Take it or leave it.'

And the guy took it, and Kiara pocketed her wad of banknotes and beamed as she saw Bryn and Alice.

'He did not,' she crowed. 'Howard did not tell me a reserve price, or that a falling to bits hay-rake was worth anything, but he did tell me that guy was a dealer. Hooray for Grandma. Hooray for me.'

She'd obviously spent the morning carting out and selling the dusty, rusty shed contents. Her hair must have been caught back to start with, but it had tugged out of its band and curls were wisping everywhere. She was wearing baggy overalls over jeans and T-shirt, and grease and rust were liberally spread. A smudge of grease lay right across her cheek and he wanted…

No. He did not want.

Liar. He wanted so badly. But she was grinning in triumph and high-fiving Alice when Alice told her she'd finished selling all Maureen's cupcakes and…

And she didn't want him.

And then a voice boomed across the crowd, that the auction of some of the more valuable goods was about to start, so Kiara closed her shed and headed over to stand under the jacaranda trees in the front yard to watch.

And Bryn and Alice stood with her and Bryn thought…

Family?

The thought almost blindsided him. What was he thinking?

But he was thinking it.

This was a woman who cared. She cared for

her lost dogs, and she cared for the little girl who stood beside her now.

'Twenty dollars feeds all our dogs for a day,' Alice had told him, and he could practically see the dollars adding up and being divided. An ancient wicker pram, surely too old to be of practical use to anyone, sold for a hundred and twenty dollars, and Alice and Kiara high-fived again.

They were having fun. *He was having fun.*

And the idea in his head was growing stronger.

There was a query about two of the auction items- could they be sold as a pair or not?- and Kiara moved away to confer with Howard. Alice went with her.

And then someone nudged him—Donna—he recognised the town's newsagent. 'Doc?'

He was busy watching Kiara thread her way through the crowd and talk to Howard. He was watching her excitement. Watching her hold Alice's hand, smiling, engaging with the kid as if she were her own. He didn't want to be distracted.

'Doc?'

The voice was more urgent and reluctantly he turned away. 'Yes?'

'Doc, it's Maureen.' Donna's face was creased in concern. 'She said she was feeling queer. I've helped her up to a seat on the veranda. She doesn't want a fuss and she's been saying she just has a headache, but now her speech is a bit funny. I don't like the way she looks.'

He frowned and turned away. As he did Kiara turned to find his face in the crowd, her beam a mile wide. They'd sold the two vases as a pair, and the price was astonishing.

He smiled back, caught in that gorgeous smile, but Donna had grasped his arm and there was no mistaking her urgency. 'Please… We need you.'

He pulled out of the crowd and limped as fast as he could over to the veranda. As he reached the steps, Kiara was suddenly back beside him.

Without Alice? He glanced back and saw Alice was at the to-be-sold table, handing something up to the auctioneer. Given a job?

What had Kiara read in his face—or Donna's face—to have her delegate so swiftly? To think of a need to delegate?

'What's wrong?' she breathed, but Donna was already hauling him up the steps and he had no time to answer.

Maureen was slumped in one of the ancient wicker chairs on the veranda. A little woman, she was dressed as she always was, in a vast flowery polyester dress that made her look a whole lot more voluminous than she really was. In honour of the occasion, she was also wearing a straw sun hat, liberally decorated with fresh daisies. A capacious apron covered her middle, its white surface showing signs of the cupcakes she'd been selling.

One hand lay limply on her thigh, and she was clutching that hand with the other. She looked… terrified.

The sounds of the crowd, Donna's presence—even Kiara's presence—dropped away as Bryn slipped back into the role he was trained for. He crouched beside her and took her hand. Her pulse was racing. 'Hey, Maureen. Donna says you have a headache.'

She tried to turn her head to see him but failed. Gently he supported her neck, holding her face so he could meet her eyes.

And also search…

'I… I dunno…' Her speech was slurred and came with a massive effort, and Bryn was already making a tentative diagnosis. As she spoke, one side of her face didn't move. The left side of her mouth had drooped.

'Can you lift your arms?' he said gently, and she gave him a look of helplessness. One arm lifted, the other didn't.

A stroke? By the look of it, a big one.

'Let's get you inside,' he told her. Her pulse was dangerously fast. Cardiac failure? 'No, don't move, I'm going to carry you.' He was unbuttoning the top of her dress as he spoke, then pulling free her tight apron ties. Her dress seemed capacious enough—a quick touch of her tummy told him there was no corset restricting things underneath. He needed to lie her down, put her in the recovery position, do a full check, but he couldn't do it here. The veranda was being used to store sold items. It was crowded with junk, and already people were turning to look up in concern.

With one easy movement he lifted her into his arms. Kiara protested—'Bryn, your leg…'—but he was stable enough to hold her. And as he did, he felt the rigidity of her panic, plus that racing heart.

'Maureen, I'm thinking you could be having a minor stroke,' he said as he held her. 'No biggie. We've caught it fast and I know what to do. You haven't had any surgery in the last few months, have you? Any accidents?'

'N… n…' She could hardly get it out.

'Have you taken aspirin for your headache? Or at any time in the last few days?'

Her eyes answered, she couldn't.

Kiara was holding the front door wide. He carried Maureen through, and Kiara was looking almost as terrified as Maureen.

He was thinking back to something Kiara had said to him when she'd introduced Maureen.

'Sometimes I think without Maureen I might fall apart.'

Kiara was a woman who'd been brought up

mostly with the same bleak childhood as his, but there had been people who loved her. Her grandmother. Maureen.

Was that what enabled her to love in return? Was that why she'd seamlessly taken the wounded Alice under her wing?

Was that why he felt…?

Enough. There was no time for examination of emotions now.

'How long have you had the headache?' he asked, and Maureen looked up at him wildly. Either she didn't understand or there was no way she could respond.

'She told Alice she had a headache almost an hour ago,' Kiara said, her voice unsteady. 'That's when Alice took over her cupcake stall. I should have…'

'There's no need for should haves,' he said, and managed a reassuring smile. 'I'm sure the last thing Maureen wanted was a fuss, isn't that right, Maureen? And she has help now. Donna, the keys to my car are in my left trouser pocket.' He was laying Maureen down on the settee, carefully supporting her limp arm. Seeing the way her left leg flopped, her foot falling limply to the side.

This was definitely a stroke, but what sort? An ischaemic stroke, caused by a blood clot, meant urgent intervention, an IV injection of a plasminogen activator—alteplase—to dissolve the clot before it could cause major, long-term brain injury. For optimum results that injection had to happen within three hours—and how long since Maureen had started displaying symptoms? An hour, when she'd first confessed to a headache? Or longer?

But he couldn't administer alteplase yet.

The alternative to an ischaemic stroke, something that could be causing similar symptoms, was a haemorrhage. If it was a haemorrhage, clot treatment would turn an emergency into a disaster.

Maureen needed state-of-the-art medical tools for diagnosis, and she needed them now.

'My car's the crimson sports coupé in the driveway.' He was talking to Donna as he thought. 'Can you grab my bag from the trunk? There's a portable defibrillator there, too, clearly marked. I doubt we'll need it but bring it anyway. Kiara, I want you to ring emergency services. Tell them who I am—a neurologist at Sydney Central. Tell them I believe Maureen's having a stroke and we need urgent assistance. Tell them sirens, speed. And I want a MICA unit to meet them—I'll talk to them if necessary.' A MICA vehicle—a mobile intensive care ambulance—would be absolutely essential if Maureen's heart was to fail under pressure.

'S...str... Am...am I...?' Maureen was trying to talk but only one side of her face was working. He was adjusting cushions, supporting her so she was lying on her side with her head slightly raised. While he worked, Kiara crouched in front of her, gripping her hands.

'It's okay, Maureen. You'll be safe. If this *is* a stroke, we have the best doctor in the world right here, isn't that right, Dr Dalton?'

And she smiled at Maureen with such love, with such assurance, that Bryn felt his breath catch. Kiara's smile would make a patient recover all by itself.

'Bryn?' Kiara's voice was reproving, and he hauled himself together. What had she said?

'Best doctor in the world'?

'Yep, I'm good,' he agreed, because there was no choice. Maureen needed reassurance. She needed to believe he knew what he was doing.

He set up a drip. He quietly asked Kiara to have the defibrillator ready. He was swiftly preparing for anything a stroke could throw at him.

He knew his medicine, but anything else? Like the way he was feeling about Kiara?

He knew nothing at all.

The two paramedics who arrived with the ambulance turned out to be young and inexperienced. The only available MICA crew was caught up on another job. Bryn therefore needed to accompany Maureen, and there was room in the ambulance for no one else.

Bryn knew that Kiara wanted—desperately—to follow in her van but she couldn't. Once Alice had realised something was wrong, she'd come running, and one look at Maureen and she'd disintegrated. Alice knew dreadful things happened, and to her this seemed yet another. Staring down at Maureen, who'd bossed her and mothered her over the last few days, she'd turned again into the solitary, white-faced child she'd been only weeks ago.

'Bryn, I'll stay,' Kiara decreed, seeing Alice's fear as soon as he did. 'I'll phone Maureen's family, and then Alice and I will look after things here. Take care of her for me, though, won't you?' Her voice trembled, but as they stretchered Maureen to the ambulance she pulled herself together.

'Right, Alice, that's Maureen, on her way to get better. I have no doubt your uncle will have her home in no time. I'll make a couple of phone calls and then we need to get back to selling stuff. Let's see how much money Maureen's cupcakes made. She'll be wanting to know that the minute her head stops hurting. How are you at counting? I'm terrible, but if we both do it, we should manage.'

The ambulance doors closed—leaving Bryn with a vision of Kiara standing in the driveway, surrounded by a crowd of concerned onlookers. Her community. Her hand was holding Alice's. Bunji was at her side.

Why that should make him feel…

And then Maureen's heart faltered and there was time for nothing but medicine. Which was the way he always wanted it.

Wasn't it?

CHAPTER ELEVEN

IT WAS AFTER midnight before Bryn walked back in the front door, and it had been a tough day. Archie had miraculously organised one locum neurologist to start work, which was supposed to have given Bryn Saturday off, but the locum was young and seemed a bit unsure—and Bryn wasn't trusting Maureen to a colleague he hardly knew.

An initial scan at the nearest hospital had confirmed the stroke was ischaemic—clotting on the brain. He'd injected alteplase—a drug that assisted in dissolving clots. Its early use could have been a lifesaver all on its own, but when they arrived at Sydney Central—a teaching hospital where stroke treatment was state-of-the-art—a further scan showed the clot wasn't dissolving fast enough.

That meant surgery—endovascular clot retrieval—and every one of his skills had to be brought to the fore.

By the time he left Theatre he was wiped.

Why?

The surgery needed hairline precision, with a woman's life at stake, so yes, the surgery was tricky, but he was used to cutting-edge surgery. He wasn't the head of the neurology department of one of Australia's top hospitals for nothing.

Normally he could turn off from the people in his care. He had to. His nerves needed to be rock steady, so during surgery he couldn't afford to think of the people under his care as...people. They could be individuals before surgery when he was assessing, informing, reassuring, and they'd be individuals afterwards when he saw them recovering in the wards. But once under anaesthetic, when every part of him needed to focus on what he was doing, they had to be technical cases, challenges to be conquered.

Today had been different. He hardly knew Maureen, but those shocked white faces—Kiara's and Alice's—had stayed with him. They'd made him see—maybe for the first time—why surgeons stood back when their own family or friends were the patients.

He'd never thought like that. He'd never thought he'd have to, but today, if there'd been someone he was sure was just as competent to call on, he would have stepped back himself.

As it was, he'd held it together. There'd been

dicey moments when Maureen's heart had faltered, but his team was good. The intervention had been early enough for him to be able to tell Maureen's anxious family that he held every hope of a full recovery.

Afterwards he'd faced the drive back to Two Tails and his leg had ached—no, all of him had ached. For some stupid reason he wasn't able to stop his hands from trembling on the steering wheel. What the hell was wrong with him?

And then he pulled into the driveway and Kiara was stepping out onto the veranda to meet him. And as he opened the car door, she came down to him in a rush, stopping for a millisecond as she reached him—and then she was folded in his arms. Her face was in his chest, he could feel her trembling—to match the trembling of his own hands—and he thought…

Maureen? Was he was shaking like a leaf over the fate of a woman he'd known for little more than a week?

No. He was shaking because Kiara loved her. Because the outcome of his surgery had never seemed so important.

His trembling had stopped now that she was folded into his arms, now that he held her close, now that his chin was on her curls. Now he was…home?

It was a weird thought, a flash among other

thoughts he couldn't process because he was too busy holding her. Hugging her. Feeling that here was…

No. With a huge effort he managed to get his voice to work.

'Hey, Kiara, it's okay. You got my phone call? There's every chance she'll make a good recovery. She has her husband with her, and her daughters. She's surrounded by people who love her, and in the best of places. You can let it go.'

But even as he said it, he knew it was wrong. He felt her stiffen, just slightly. But still she held, still her face was buried in his chest, still she was taking the comfort she so obviously needed.

'Maureen was pretty much my grandma's only friend,' she said, her voice muffled because she wasn't moving from his chest. 'Grandma was a loner, but Maureen just barged in and cared. When I came here as a little girl, Maureen was a constant. She's my friend, like Hazel is my friend.' She took a deep breath and pushed away a little, just enough so she could say what she needed to say. 'She's pretty much all the family I have.'

And what was there in that that made his gut lurch? That made him want to tug her back tighter against him. That made him want to say…

No. The sensations he was feeling now were almost overwhelming, but he had enough sense to realise he needed to keep his head. He had a sudden memory of a nanny, employed for almost four years from when he'd been three to when he was seven. Of his father telling him that they were moving, and Gloria would be leaving.

'There'll be a new nanny during holidays, and you'll be at boarding school most of the time anyway. Only babies make a fuss.'

Why that memory now? Why the almost instinctive muscle memory to pull himself into himself, to brace…

'C-come in.' Kiara was visibly tugging herself together, pulling away, swiping her eyes. 'Oh, thank God you were here, Bryn, but you must be exhausted. There's a gorgeous rich soup that Maureen made for us…' She choked a little on that but bit her lip and turned back to the house, leaving him to follow. 'She'll give us a hard time if we waste it, so let's get it into you and then get some sleep.'

The house was still a muddle after the sale, packing boxes, furniture shoved aside so things could be moved easily, mess. The kitchen was cluttered, but the smell of the soup was warmly welcoming.

'The mess is for tomorrow,' Kiara said wearily as she poured two bowls. 'I'll eat with you if you don't mind. Alice ate before she went to bed—she loved the soup, and she was so tired and proud of what she did today—but I couldn't eat until I heard from you.'

And then, because it seemed the only obvious place to go, they headed once again for the open fire in the living room. She'd obviously built it up during the long hours of waiting, sitting by the flames, taking comfort from its warmth.

'Bunji should be with you,' he told her, because the thought of her sitting here alone, waiting for news of her friend, was adding to emotions he was struggling to understand.

'Bunji's Alice's dog now,' she said firmly, and managed a tired smile. 'And Alice needed her. She was frightened about Maureen, but we counted our loot—wow, we did well, by the way—then she took Bunji off to a quiet part of the garden and told her all about it. I watched them as everyone left and…it helped. That they're content. That she has Bunji she can talk to.'

He nodded, thinking it through. Hearing the note of strain in her voice. Still remembering the sensation of that hug, of her walking into his arms and holding on.

'So who do you turn to when you need to talk?'

'Same as you, I guess,' she said simply. 'We've learned to be independent.'

'Sometimes independence sucks.'

'Does it?' she asked curiously. 'Don't you need it?'

He didn't answer. He found he couldn't.

The answer should have been obvious. Yes, he valued his independence. It'd been instilled into him since birth, to rely on himself and himself alone, and it was all he knew. But there was something about this night. Something about this woman…

She wasn't waiting for a response. She addressed herself instead to her bowl of soup and left him to silence.

She was letting him be. Respecting his need for space. For his precious independence.

She always would, he thought. All her animals, all her clients—she spent her life figuring who needed what, and then fixing it for them. Alice was healing because of Kiara. Even him… Yeah, he'd been floundering when Kiara had come into his life, but she'd pretty much sorted it. She'd invited them into her home while Alice had bonded with Bunji, she'd allowed him to resume his career without feeling guilty, she'd encouraged his fledgling relationship with his niece. She'd figured a way they could all move forward.

But what about Kiara? He looked around at the stripped living room. She'd obviously gone overboard with her yard sale and the place looked barren. Almost everything had been sold. What he'd paid her, combined with what she'd earned by today's sale, would surely enable her to keep Two Tails running for a good while longer. Even if it didn't, then she must surely agree to let him help even more.

But the thought of her living on here alone…

He'd been shocked when he'd walked back in tonight. He'd expected her to sell things she hadn't needed, but she'd taken it to extremes. No wonder she was pleased with her takings—she'd practically stripped the place bare.

It was still liveable, but without her grandmother's clutter, stripped to the bones of furniture…did it look like a home any longer?

Home?

Why did that word keep surfacing?

It was tied, almost inextricably, with Kiara.

He thought of her as he'd seen her when he'd left with Maureen. She'd been standing in the driveway, holding Alice's hand. With a battered dog at her feet. With a community around her…

Home.

An idea was stirring—or maybe it had stirred already but it was growing stronger by the minute.

A plan?

But overriding his embryonic plan was the

sensation that he wanted to be closer to this woman, and he wanted it right now.

She finished her soup and set her bowl aside, then looked queryingly up at him. He'd sunk into one of the two remaining armchairs, but she'd settled on the rug, closer to the fire. 'Finished?' she asked. 'Bed?'

'It sounds good to me,' he said, a trifle unsteadily, and he set his bowl carefully with hers and then reached down and traced her cheekbone with his finger. 'You need to sleep, too.'

'I'm not sure I can.' And she lifted her hand and covered his.

There was a long silence, a silence while the world seemed to hold it breath. Her hand was warm on his, and his fingers cupped her face. The link seemed to be strengthening by the minute. The pull.

The need to be close.

And then he kissed her.

She'd kissed him before—twice. They hadn't been...kisses, though. They'd meant something to him, but he'd told himself they'd just been a part of Kiara's warmth, Kiara's need to comfort.

There was no way this kiss was about comfort. This kiss was about...everything.

The culmination of a hell of a day? The culmination of months of hell?

No. This kiss was so much more. As her mouth

met his, as she twisted and knelt so she could sink into the kiss, as the contact melded and burned…

This was about nothing but them. A man and a woman and pure physical desire.

And maybe even more than that.

It was a kiss like he'd never experienced. A kiss that seemed a joining, an affirmation of an aching need to be closer, closer than he'd ever felt with another soul.

She was in his arms now, holding him as he was holding her. He could feel her desire matching his. Oh, this woman… Kiara…

His…love?

The word terrified him—had always terrified him—but right now it seemed the only one available. But he'd think about it later. Right now, there was only Kiara, only this moment, only this kiss.

And when the kiss ended—as even the best kisses must inevitably end—when he finally managed to speak, he hardly recognised his voice. It was deep, husky, aching with want.

The way she was holding him…the warmth of her…the sheer loveliness… He could scarcely make his voice work, but somehow, he said it. 'Kiara, I won't take advantage of you but if you…'

He paused. He had no right to say this, no right to ask.

But she was gazing back up at him, her eyes inches from him, wide, honest, meeting his gaze head on.

'You're asking?' Amazingly her smile emerged again. Half teasing. Half tender.

'It's your house,' he said, feeling helpless because he was way out of his comfort zone. He wouldn't—couldn't—push this woman when he owed her so much.

When he wanted her so much.

'Your house,' he managed again, and his hand was cupping her chin, his eyes locked on hers. 'Your rules.'

'Then hooray for that,' she said, and for heaven's sake, the teasing note was uppermost again. 'Bryn, I've been wanting to jump your body for days now—no, make that weeks. And it's dumb, you're my client and I'm old enough to know that mixing business with pleasure is a disaster, but you're leaving soon and…'

'And?'

'And I think you'd better kiss me again,' she told him, and her hand gripped his even more firmly. Strong and sure. This was a woman who'd made a decision. Who knew what she wanted and had every intention of taking it.

'If you want me,' she said simply, 'I'm sleeping in my grandma's bed and it's a double. There's no pressure, Bryn. No expectations, no claims on a future, but we're both grown up and we've had one hell of a day. So for tonight… It would be my very great pleasure to share.'

Whoops.

That probably wasn't the most romantic thought to wake to, but it was there, front and centre, a great, fat thought bubble the moment she opened her eyes to daylight.

She did, however, wake gloriously. There was no denying that last night had been extraordinary. She'd fallen into Bryn's arms, probably out of exhaustion, or a surfeit of emotion, or relief. But lust had played a big part, too, and sense had taken a back seat. She'd practically invited him into her bed—okay, she *had* invited him into her bed, and maybe it had been worth every moment of whatever the consequences would be.

There shouldn't be any, she told herself. She'd had brief relationships in the past, and surely the guy she'd slept with was experienced? They both knew what they were doing. The sex had been mind-blowingly good. It had been a fabulous night, blasting everything apart from physical need out of both of their minds.

So why had she woken thinking *Whoops*?

Because she'd also woken up feeling as if she wouldn't mind staying exactly where she was for the rest of her life.

And that was crazy. There'd been no commitment on either side, and neither should there be. Soon Bryn would leave. His new housekeeper had been employed. Alice would start at her new school in Clovelly and life would restart for all of them.

With the money she'd earned she could keep Two Tails going a while longer. Maybe there'd be other avenues of fundraising. She'd been running on the smell of an oily rag for years now, and she'd just keep going.

By herself.

No, she told herself firmly, managing to think it through, even though she was spooned into the curve of Bryn's body, even though the warmth, the strength of him were a siren call that was melting something within. She wouldn't be by herself. She'd have her dogs. She'd have Maureen back again. She'd have Hazel's friendship, she'd have her community, she'd…

Not have Bryn.

Which wouldn't matter. There was no need at all for her to lie here and think *Whoops*. The whoops was because of the way he made her feel—as if everything she needed in life was right here, in the curve of his body, in the way he held her, loved her…

He didn't love her. That thought blindsided her and also…the way she felt about him.

What was she doing, falling for a rich, arrogant, self-centred doctor who was nothing to do with her world?

Except she sort of had, and there was little she could do about it except think… *Whoops.*

He stirred and his arms firmed around her. She wriggled around to face him, looping her arms around his neck and kissing him as he woke—because a woman would have to be inhuman to do otherwise. And when he smiled at her, when his eyes were inches from hers, when his gorgeous body responded, and heat and desire flared all over again…

Whoops indeed, but the time to cope with the future… Well, that was for the future.

'Good morning, my love,' he murmured as he gathered her against him and their worlds merged into a glorious moment of pure, animal bliss.

'It's a very good morning,' she whispered back.

Despite the whoops.

The world had to break in, and it broke in soon.

A group of locals arrived to give Kiara a hand clearing up the mess from yesterday's sale, sorting stuff that had been sold, generally turning the day into a working bee. The yard sale itself had generated interest, but Maureen's collapse had tapped into community concern. Kiara was surrounded.

Bryn needed to head back to Sydney Central to check on Maureen. Yes, his new locum was more than capable of doing what was needed, but he needed to clear his head.

He needed to think about the plan that had half formed the night before.

Last night had been life changing. Last night had dispersed any doubts he'd had about his embryonic idea. It was starting to seem brilliant, from every angle he looked at it.

There were problems, he conceded, but they were minor. Two Tails was a fair distance from Sydney Central. Almost an hour's drive was too much when he worked six days a week, with call-backs in emergencies. Could he commute? Would Kiara consider moving her premises somewhere closer? His house at Clovelly wouldn't work, he conceded that, but somewhere else…

They'd work it out together, he thought.

If she agreed.

And the thought came suddenly, the question seeming like a kick in the guts. 'What if she doesn't agree?'

It didn't matter, he told himself. The alternative was surely going on as they'd organised. Plan A had always been to take take Alice back to Clovelly, to depend on his new housekeeper for out-of-school care, to get on with his independent life. The idea of combining his and Kiara's life…yeah, it had advantages, especially for Alice, but surely it was Plan B.

Except it wasn't. He'd woken with Kiara in his arms, and he'd felt…as he'd never felt before. As he'd never expected to feel.

As if he wanted to spend the rest of his life with this woman in his arms.

And that was a dumb thought. His independence was everything. The thought of needing her…

No. This wasn't need—at least, not *his* need. It couldn't be. All the lessons he'd learned throughout his isolated childhood, every time he'd sworn not to get attached…those rules had been rammed home with pain that was bone deep. The thought of opening himself to that level of exposure was unthinkable. He couldn't go there.

But Plan B was practical as well as desirable, he told himself, shoving emotion aside. Alice and Kiara could be gloriously happy together. Kiara would allow him to fund Two Tails into the future and every night when he came home…

Yeah, that was like a siren's song.

But it was still sensible, and he needed to be sensible. So… Where to go from here?

Should he buy a diamond and do the romantic bit?

No. He thought of Kiara's teasing smile, he thought of himself down on one knee and thought she'd probably break into laughter.

He smiled at the vision.

'She's just as sensible as I am,' he said out loud as he drove. 'Just as independent. Just as aware of long-term advantages. If she'd like a diamond, of course she can have one, but this will be on her terms. As my part of the contract will be on my terms.'

It did sound sensible but there was a part of him that wasn't feeling very sensible. The part of him that had woken with Kiara in his arms and had felt as if sensible was…melting.

'Hold it together,' he told himself roughly. 'If you let emotion get in the way of sensible, she'll be the first to back away. We both know the rules.'

And then he was turning into the hospital car park and the world of medicine enclosed him again.

Which was the way he liked it. A world where he could spend his life trying to fix chaos.

A world where he didn't risk exposing his own life to the same.

CHAPTER TWELVE

WHAT FOLLOWED FOR Kiara was a week that was almost dreamlike. Time out of frame. The following Monday Alice would start at her new school, so on the Saturday Bryn would take Alice and Bunji back to Clovelly. The new housekeeper was already installed, and Bryn had taken both Kiara and Alice over to meet her. Alice had been quiet and clinging to Kiara, but she'd come back to Two Tails seemingly resigned.

'I can come back here sometimes,' she'd said wistfully to Kiara, and Kiara had hugged her and told her of course she could.

For as long as Two Tails kept running.

Even then she'd stay in touch, she thought. In the short time she'd known her, she'd been stunned with the connection she felt. Alice's isolation was yet another mirror of her own childhood.

As, it seemed, of Bryn's.

And there, too, was a connection. More than a connection. The way she was starting to feel…

When he'd arrived back from the hospital on the Sunday, after that first night in her shared bed, she'd felt like a woman after her first ever sexual encounter. She'd felt almost absurdly shy, and anxious, and unsure where the relationship could go.

She'd also been frightened, as she'd been waiting to hear how…if… Maureen was recovering.

But on his return, he'd walked back into the kitchen, seen her look of fear and gathered her into his arms.

'She's conscious,' he'd told her. 'We've put her back to sleep now—an induced coma will give her an easier route to complete healing—but we let her stir for a little while I was there. She knew her family. She even managed to murmur her husband's name, and at this stage it's more than promising that there'll be no long-term damage.'

Such a relief! He'd held her while her world seemed to settle, and then Alice had edged close, and she'd somehow been included in the hug. And Bunji had barked, and they'd looked down and the expression on the dog's face—they could have sworn it was jealousy. They'd ended up laughing and Bryn had picked Bunji up and hugged her, too, and Kiara had felt…

Well, she'd felt as she had for a week now.

As if things were happening she didn't understand. Yes, Bryn and Alice were due to leave, but every night she lay in Bryn's arms, and as the date to leave grew closer a huge question started to loom.

She didn't dare hope, but the way he held her…

How did a woman stop dreaming?

'How's it going?' Her friend, Hazel, rang halfway through the week. Hazel had been busy since Kiara had last seen her, and when she rang, she seemed almost dazed. The story had escalated. Her boss…the baby… Kiara was scarcely able to take in the events that had overtaken her friend, and then she had to struggle to find words to describe what was going on in her own life.

'I think… I'm not sure…' she started, and Hazel was astute enough to hear behind the words.

'So you and Bryn…'

'Hazel, I don't know,' she said honestly.

'You're sleeping with him?'

'Yes.' There'd never been any way she could lie to Hazel.

'Are you in love with him?'

And how could she lie about something like this? 'I think I am.' Then she corrected herself. 'No. I definitely am. The way he makes me feel… But Hazel…'

'You don't know how *he* feels?'

'He holds me like he means it.'

'But you don't know?'

'It's just…he's been a loner for such a long time. I know he cares. I think…he wants to take care of me.'

'That sounds a bit like a one-way deal.'

'I'd take care of him.'

'Like one of your dogs?' It was meant as a joke. Hazel said it lightly, but Kiara suddenly had a vision of herself, caring for Bunji. And she thought…was that how Bryn saw her? As a woman he could somehow save?

Why did she think that? They were equals, weren't they? A man and a woman who could become friends as well as lovers.

She was growing to depend on him, she thought, with weird self-knowledge. The way she felt when she saw him leave in the mornings… The way she felt as she listened for his car returning every night…

There was a long silence and then Hazel, who knew her so well that maybe she could even read silence, said gently, 'Oh, love, don't let your heart get broken.'

'That's crazy.' She said it strongly but strong wasn't how she was feeling. 'We're mature adults. Whatever we work out…'

'Working out doesn't sound like happy ever after.'

'Which you've found?'

Somehow she managed to change direction, to get Hazel to talk about her own happiness. The conversation ended. The kennels needed cleaning and dogs needed walking. Alice and Bunji were bouncing beside her, and reservations could be held at bay.

Three more days until Saturday. And then?

Whatever happened would happen, she told herself. She could accept it.

And the way she felt about Bryn?

She could not break her heart.

She would not!

Friday.

Bryn managed to finish work early. He came home to find his girls digging in the veggie garden, preparing a new tomato bed.

His girls… As his idea had progressed, more and more he'd felt the feeling of proprietorship grow. It scared him but he accepted it.

Into the mix of emotions that had been battering his world since the night his sister died had come Kiara. Gorgeous, courageous, caring Kiara.

His girls?

His woman.

It was an emotion that was almost primeval,

inappropriate, surely, but the feeling he had for her…

Well, maybe it was primeval. Inevitable.

And the way their bodies responded to each other? Surely she had to agree?

They were digging compost into newly cleared beds, and they were both filthy. Most of the remaining dogs in the pens had been let out to join them. Bunji was digging as well—at last there were no dressings, no wounds that could reinfect—and she was glorying in being just a pup.

Being cared for. Being loved.

He'd take care of them all, he swore, and he smiled as he saw the trays of tomato seedlings waiting to go in. Three weeks ago, Kiara had been preparing to sell this place. Now she was looking at the future.

'If I'm careful I think I have enough funds to keep me going for a year,' she'd said proudly the night before, and he thought, what he was about to say would extend that indefinitely.

Bunji would have a home. Alice would have someone who cared, someone who made her laugh, someone she could hug. Kiara would be able to care for as many waifs and strays as she wanted.

And him…

He could keep doing the work he loved. He

wouldn't lose his independence, but whenever he wanted they'd be here for him.

His girls.

They'd seen him now. Alice waved a loaded shovel and then squealed as the load slid down her front. Then she giggled.

Kiara just straightened and smiled—and that smile was a smile a man could come home to for the rest of his life.

It was strange but the thought was vaguely unsettling. The rest of his life?

'How's Maureen?' It was Alice, and she asked the question every time he came home. In the week they'd spent together the two seemed to have forged a close connection. People come… people go…

What he was proposing was for the rest of his life? The thought was huge. How to get his head around it?

'She's great,' he managed. 'She's still a bit wobbly but she should be home in a couple of weeks.'

'But I won't be here,' Alice whispered, and there was the echo of the scared little girl again. 'Can I go and see her?'

'Maybe in a week or so.'

'Is she very far?'

'She's in my hospital.' He turned and gestured across the massive ravine at the back of the house, over the untamed bushland that was part of Australia's Blue Mountains. 'If there weren't so many trees, we could almost see Maureen from here. Tonight look out your window and you'll see the lights across the valley. Maybe Maureen will be standing at her window, looking at our lights.'

'Oh,' Alice said in a small voice, and Kiara stooped to hug her.

'But you will see her. I promise.'

And once again he was caught by how easily this caring business seemed to come to her. How amazing she was.

She needed to be amazing. This was the woman he hoped to be with…for ever?

And there was that gut-lurch again.

The thought of forever seemed like some sort of chasm, and he had no idea what it held. But in his pocket was a diamond—yeah, he'd had second thoughts because he needed Kiara to see he was serious. For in his head was a serious plan. A sensible plan.

This was no moment for qualms. He was committed to Alice anyway. He was…stuck.

That was hardly an appropriate thought for a man about to propose marriage, he thought wryly, but there were so many compensations. This woman, hugging his niece, smiling at Alice until she smiled back, then smiling up at him.

This woman, with dirt on her nose, with dogs at her heels.

She was wonderful.

She was independent. She wouldn't cling.

She was surely perfect.

'I've ordered dinner in,' he said, struggling to move to the practical. He'd thought he ought to take Kiara out, but organising someone to care for Alice would never work. Maureen, maybe, but with Maureen still in hospital his planned romantic dinner had to be at home.

Home. The idea was still unsettling. He knew Kiara loved this place, but it wasn't ideal. Could he talk her into moving? If they found acreage closer, he could talk to the architect who'd designed his place. Something a bit cutting edge. She'd want her dogs, of course—they'd have to be part of the deal—so it'd have to be remote enough not to bother neighbours, but money could solve most problems.

But that was for the future. Kiara's smile was high beam. 'An order-in dinner? It'll cost heaps to get it delivered out here but if you're sure… I could take a long bath instead of cooking. That's only one step below you cooking for us.'

Him cook? He'd never thought… But it hadn't been meant as a jibe. She was still beaming. 'I'd hug you,' she told him, 'but I'd get compost over your suit. That has to be Italian, surely. Did I ever tell you how smooth you look? You fit in here like a pig in a parlour. Just lucky you're heading home tomorrow. Alice, you want first bath or me? Toss you for it, heads or tails…'

'I don't want to go home,' Alice said in a small voice.

'Yeah, well, I have an idea about that,' Kiara said briskly. 'Once you're at school we might organise you a weekend job. How about every Saturday you and Bunji come out here and help with the dogs? I can collect you if your uncle can't bring you. For as long as Two Tails stays open, and even after, you'll still be my friend.'

'I guess. But I'll still miss you.'

'And I'll miss you, but instead of thinking about it, let's have bubble baths.' And they headed to the house hand in hand, heading to serial baths.

Kiara had partially solved Alice's immediate distress, he thought as he watched them go. But his solution was better.

It was better for them all. All Kiara had to do was agree.

He'd gone all out with his dinner order, and it was delicious. Thai food. Crunchy spring rolls filled with garden-fresh sprouts and seasoning. Tiny skewers—meat on sticks—with a chilli dipping sauce. Then dish after dish of gorgeous, fragrant concoctions that had all of them eating more than they thought they could. Even Alice. He watched her agonise over the last skewer and finally decide she had to be able to fit it in. The change to this little girl had been miraculous.

And then Alice yawned and kissed them both goodnight and there was another miracle all by itself. She was still a little teary about the thought of leaving in the morning, but she seemed resigned. Then he and Kiara settled on the rug by the fire, with half a bottle of champagne left between them—and the time was right.

Now or never.

'Kiara...' he began, and thought, How does a guy just come out and say these things? He'd heard of naff proposals in his time—banners flying from aeroplanes, romantic balloon rides and proposals at a thousand feet, declarations of devotion on stage in front of a crowd that would pressure a woman to accept, no matter what her inclination was...

It was surely better this way, he thought. In Kiara's own space.

He felt a sudden shaft of uncertainty. In his pocket was a crimson box with a solitaire diamond. Maybe he had jumped the gun on this. Would it be applying more pressure?

Quit it with the qualms, he told himself and took a slug of champagne—and said it.

'Kiara.' He cleared his throat and tried again. 'I'd like… I think it might work for both of us if you'd marry me.'

There. The thing was said. Not romantic but sensible. Given the way their bodies responded to each other, given their circumstances, surely it was a reasonable proposal? So why did it feel loaded?

The fire crackled behind them, but the silence behind it felt like a ten-ton weight. Or warnings of an avalanche, ready to crash from a height?

They were leaning on cushions wedged against the armchairs. The firelight was playing on their faces. The bottle of champagne was between them.

Maybe he should have chosen somewhere less intimate?

Kiara was looking at Bryn in astonishment. Then, very carefully, she shifted the champagne—and their glasses—out of his reach.

'We've slept together for less than a week and now you're thinking we should get married?' She spoke slowly—as if not wishing to fire up a lunatic? 'You're never serious.'

'I'm serious.'

'You can't be.'

'I believe I am.'

'Why?'

'It's sensible.'

'Sensible?'

'Yes.'

There was a long silence while she seemed to struggle to get her thoughts in order. It took a while.

'Bryn, it's been a great week,' she said at last. 'An awesome few weeks, if I'm honest. I've loved being with you. I love that you've helped me. I love the way you're starting to love Alice, and I love that you're getting your life back on track. I've also enjoyed the sex—truthfully, it's been amazing. But us? Great as this time has been, you don't want to get married.'

'I think I do.' He was feeling faintly absurd. Totally off balance. 'But that's supposed to be your line.'

'I don't.'

'Really?' Her reaction wasn't in the script. Nor was the look of distress he was starting to see.

'Bryn, no.'

'Why not?' This wasn't going well. He had to explain. 'Kiara, hear me out. We're both in trouble. You're financially strapped and you're alone.'

'I'm not. I have friends…'

'You have a community, yes, and you have Hazel and Maureen. But from what you've been telling me Hazel's caught up in her own concerns. Maureen's elderly and she won't be around for ever. You're too busy to get closer to anyone else. You'll be left…'

'A crazy old lady, surrounded by her dogs?' She managed a wobbly smile. 'That sounds like a threat.'

'It's not meant to be. It's just practicality. I know you'll manage alone—as will Alice and I—but couldn't it be better for all of us if we work things out together?'

She looked into his eyes, as if trying to read what was behind his words. 'What you're proposing sounds like a house-share arrangement. You're talking marriage?'

'It *is* sensible.'

'"Sensible" is house-sharing. "Sensible" is a short-term arrangement for convenience. Surely marriage isn't meant to be…*sensible*?'

'Then it should be,' he said. 'For my parents, yours too, for that matter, not being sensible meant disaster. From what I've seen, emotion and impulsiveness remove the ability to make sensible decisions.'

'So you're not saying that you've fallen in love with me?' And her voice wobbled a little as she said it.

And what was it in that tremulous wobble that had him wanting to gather her into his arms, right there and then, as he'd held her for these last wonderful nights? He wanted her face buried in his chest. He wanted to tell her she was loved, and he'd love her. For always. The full romantic bit.

What was holding him back?

But the old fears were there, the certainties battered in from birth. He couldn't lie. He couldn't make a promise he might well not be able to keep.

He surely felt about her as he felt about no other woman, but his life was still out there, his independence, his freedom. If he let himself go one step further, if he let his emotions take him where they willed, then he'd be wide open. Exposed. His previous life was still with him, lessons instilled, reinforced and reinforced again.

'Kiara, we're fond of each other…'

'Fond!'

'More than fond,' he conceded. 'The way I feel about you… I want you.'

'In your bed.'

'Yes.' There was no reason why he shouldn't be honest.

'But not in your life. You'd still work crazy hours. Medicine would be your life.'

'And you'd still run Two Tails.'

'And Alice would fit in the cracks in the middle?'

'There'll be Maureen,' he said, feeling out of his depth. What was she expecting him to say—

that he become a part-time parent? He wasn't a parent. 'Plus we'd have a housekeeper. We could also hire a nanny if you think Alice needs it.'

She was looking at him in horror and he didn't get it. What else did she want from him?

That he be a part-time husband? He'd do what he could, but surely other couples fitted their love lives around their careers.

'You don't really want either of us,' she said, and her words were bleak, as if she was stating the inevitable.

'I do want you.'

'But Alice?'

'I have Alice, whether I want her or not.'

'Oh, for heaven's sake... Listen to yourself.' She was angry now, flushed, furious. 'Alice is your niece. You're all she has in the world.'

'Okay.' He was so out of his depth he was no longer sure what he was saying. 'I do want her...'

'But she'll be easier if you have a wife.'

'That's not what I meant.'

'Then what do you mean?'

'Just...that we could make a great family. You and me and Alice and Bunji.' He was floundering and he knew it. 'Maybe even another child if you wanted.'

'If I wanted?' There was no mistaking the anger now. 'I? Not you. Not *us*.'

'It's just that...'

'It wouldn't have very much to do with you, would it? Because your family responsibilities would be taken over by me, by Maureen, by your housekeeper and maybe a nanny. Tell me, Bryn, if you didn't have Alice, would you want me?'

'I wouldn't have met you.'

'That's not what I'm asking. Does sleeping in my bed, in my arms, count for nothing?'

Emotion had never been his forte—indeed, he'd learned to quash it. He could cope when confronted with tearful patients or emotional relatives, but on his own turf? With the woman he'd decided to marry? He was really struggling.

And now her voice was cold. 'I imagine this proposal is because I tick off most boxes for suitability,' she said bleakly. 'Good with children. Tick. Can help train Bunji. Tick. Likes Alice. Double tick. Has a career so won't get in your way too much. Good in bed. How many ticks are we up to?'

'Kiara…'

'I don't get it.' She was now sounding ineffably weary. 'But it *is* like one of your medical forms. I seem to have ticked enough of the boxes, so I win a wedding to the wonderful Bryn Dalton.'

'There's no need to be offensive.'

'Isn't there?' She shook her head, her eyes bleak. 'Sorry, Bryn, no.'

'Is that all you can say?'

'To a very generous offer? Yes, it is. Enough.' She rose and headed for the door but then she turned back. 'You see, Bryn,' she said, in a voice that was now full of pain, 'I have a problem. Somehow over the last weeks I've managed the impossible. I've actually fallen in love.'

'Then...'

'Then nothing.' The pain was almost tangible. 'Because your contract would be totally one-sided. I'd love Bunji, I'd love Alice, and yes, I'd love you. And you...you'd do what you thought was necessary to make us all happy.'

'Couldn't that be enough?'

'There's not one snowball's chance in a bushfire it'd be enough,' she retorted. 'I might be emotionally challenged but I know that much—I'd end up breaking my heart.'

'But why?'

'Because you don't care,' she flashed. 'Not really, not so deeply in your gut that it's a visceral thing. And I know you don't get it, and it's not worth me trying even to explain. So tomorrow you take Alice home and you get on as best you can with the love you're prepared to give.'

'Kiara, I don't know how to love her any more than I already do.'

'Don't you want her?'

'I don't know,' he said, honestly. 'If there was any other way...'

'Well, you'd better make your mind up pretty fast,' she said brutally. 'Your plan to have me take over loving hasn't worked. She's a great kid. I'd keep her myself if there was any way Two Tails could make enough to support more than one of us, but I can't. So it's up to you, and she deserves more.'

'I know it, but I can't...'

'Or won't,' she said bluntly. 'Loving's easy, Bryn. You just have to open your heart and trust.'

'But you won't.'

'It's a two-way deal,' she told him. 'Sorry, Bryn, nice try but I'm going to bed.'

And she walked out and closed the door behind her.

But upstairs...

Alice had settled into bed, but she hadn't slept. The thought of leaving in the morning was too huge. She lay and stared into the dark, and then Bunji had stirred at her feet and started to whine.

And she remembered she'd forgotten her water bowl.

Bunji was supposed to drink downstairs—that was the rule—but her leg was sore and it'd take two minutes to head down to the bathroom on the next level and fill her bowl. And as she did, she heard voices floating up from the open living-room door.

'Don't you want her?' That was Kiara—talking about her?

'I don't know,' Bryn was saying. *'If there was any other way...'*

The words made her freeze.

Somehow, in all the awfulness of the last few months, she'd never doubted that her uncle wanted her. Hadn't he climbed down the cliff to save her?

Wouldn't he want her to stay with him—wherever he was—for ever?

'Don't you want her?'

'I don't know.'

Something cold felt as if it were squeezing her insides. Something vicious, something searingly painful. Bunji, who'd crept down with her, put her soft head against her knee and snuffled.

She hugged her dog, but all she could feel was pain. If Bryn didn't want her, what would he do with her? Send her to this unknown school he'd told her about? But she'd still have to stay at his place at nights and on weekends. The boarding school, then, the one Aunt Beatrice had insisted on?

Kiara?

The voices floated on from downstairs.

Kiara couldn't afford to keep her.

For a moment she thought she might vomit,

but then she hauled herself together. A solitary childhood had left her resourceful.

She was thinking suddenly of one of the last times she'd seen Maureen. They'd been making cupcakes for the yard sale.

'They're brilliant,' Maureen had said of Alice's colourful creations, and she'd hugged her. 'You're so precious. If you were my grandy I'd take you home in a heartbeat.'

'Really?'

'Really. My daughters have left home, and I've always wanted a granddaughter like you.'

Maureen.

The more she thought about it, the more it made sense. Kiara couldn't keep her. Her uncle didn't want her. Maureen did.

So where was Maureen? She was struggling to remember what Bryn had said.

'She's in my hospital.' He'd gestured across the valley, across the untamed bushland that was part of Australia's Blue Mountains. *'If there weren't so many trees, we could almost see Maureen from here.'*

Maureen was recovering in Sydney Central Hospital. Bryn's hospital.

She crept along the passage until she came to the bathroom. Here, on the second level, balancing on the toilet seat, she could gaze down the valley, over the moonlit mountains, over the tops of the mass of bushland and to the great glow in the distance that was Sydney.

Specifically, Sydney Central.

She knew hospitals—her mother had been in and out of them with drug overdoses many times in Alice's short life. They were easy enough to navigate. You just went to the front desk, told them you wanted to see your mother, and someone would appear and take you to see her. Or explain very nicely why you couldn't. With her mom that'd been because she was being crazy, and Maureen wouldn't be crazy.

Maureen would want her.

So all she had to do was head for the lights, find the hospital—surely everyone would know where Sydney Central was—and then ask to see her… her what? What would she call Maureen?

Grandmother, she decided, and the idea pleased her. She'd love a grandma.

And Maureen would hug her again—she knew she would—and she'd take her home because Maureen really wanted her.

Someone had to want her.

She sniffed but then swallowed and decided not to cry. She'd done enough of that, and she had a plan.

She'd need to pack a little food—it seemed a long way to the lights. And she'd also take Bunji. Bunji was her friend, and she wouldn't be so alone if she had Bunji. It'd take courage, but with Bunji she thought she could do it. She was brave, and it was a good plan.

And if it worked, she wouldn't need to bother Kiara—or Bryn—ever again.

Why had she bothered to go to bed at all? Kiara lay and stared at the ceiling and tried to figure why she'd knocked back…an offer too good to refuse?

For in the bleakness of the night, without Bryn's body to warm her, that was what it seemed like. A magical offer. A happy-ever-after. Kiara and Bryn and Alice: security for them all, Two Tails for ever. Maybe even a baby. Sometimes in her quiet times she'd found herself aching for a child of her own. So why couldn't her dream include Bryn? A friend, a lover, a husband.

But what Bryn was offering was all on his terms. Financial security. Friendship. But only when he wasn't working or studying or at conferences. She knew full well that the only reason she'd seen so much of him up until now was because he'd hurt his leg.

So what was left? Passion? Probably yes, but even there, love didn't come into the equation.

She knew Bryn well enough now to realise what he felt for her was probably as strong as it was going to get. Even that emotion had surprised him, she decided. He'd proposed with the air of a man doing a business deal.

So…he needed her for practical reasons. He was stuck with Alice, and he was arranging his ducks in a row so he could get his life back into the order he so valued. He might even end up being a decent husband and father. He'd do his best and his best would keep them safe. Maybe even contented? He was talented, he was devoted…

No. He was devoted to his work. To his independence.

Marriage to her would mean he had more independence, not less. The thought left her feeling so bleak she shivered.

Maybe she should go fetch one of her dogs for comfort, she thought, as the night wore on and sleep was nowhere, but teaching dogs to sleep on beds was not in her training scheme. She thought of Bunji, who'd probably be in bed with Alice. That had to be one happy ending.

Alice and Bunji…happy ever after.

Why did that thought make her lonelier still?

CHAPTER THIRTEEN

SHE WAS SCRUBBING the kennels when Bryn came to find her the next morning. Not that they needed scrubbing, but she had to do something. She'd been up since dawn, edgy and unhappy, and here in the kennels, chatting to the last of her resident dogs, she could find a kind of peace.

Today Bryn and Alice would be leaving. With the cheque she'd receive for services rendered she could reopen the empty pens. She could hire someone to help her until Maureen was fit enough to come back. She could move on.

She'd done a great job these last weeks, uniting one sad dog with one bereft child. She should be over the moon.

Instead she was scrubbing and swearing—and occasionally pausing to swipe a sleeve across her eyes.

And then the pen door swung open. Bryn's beautiful brogues were suddenly at foot level. Uh oh. She sniffed and swiped her face a couple more times before she hauled herself up to face him.

'It's the disinfectant,' she said, and for the life of her she couldn't stop herself sounding defensive. 'It makes my eyes water.'

He handed her a handkerchief—oh, for heaven's sake, it was linen. She repaid his generosity by blowing her nose and pocketing it.

'I'll post it back washed,' she told him.

'Keep it.'

'Then deduct it from my pay.'

'Kiara...'

'Let's get this over with,' she said roughly. 'Are you packed? Where's Alice?'

'I assumed she was out here with you.'

'I haven't seen her.' She frowned. For the last few days, the little girl had been bouncing out of bed at the first sound of anyone stirring. This morning she'd assumed she was in the house with Bryn. 'Maybe she's just savouring her last morning in the attic.'

But she saw unease on Bryn's face at the same time she felt it herself, and wordlessly they made their way back to the house. Up to the attic.

With Bryn still limping—he should still be using his cane—Kiara beat him to the top of the stairs. She knocked. 'Alice?'

Nothing.

Her heart did a stupid lurch. Maybe she was

out in the garden, she told herself. Feeding the chooks one last time? But surely, she would have seen…

She knocked again and entered.

No Alice. No Bunji. Just a bed, carefully made, and a note lying on the coverlet.

Dear Kiara

I heard you and Bryn talking last night. I know you can't afford to keep me, and Bryn doesn't want me, but Maureen does. She tells me all the time.

She says, 'You're just like my grown-up girls. My house is so empty now. I'd love it if I could take you home with me.'

Maureen kisses me and hugs me, and I like it. Bryn says she's getting better, so I'm going to find her and ask. If she says no, then I'll have to stay with Bryn, but Bunji and I want to try.

Bryn says it's just over the mountains. I saw the glow last night. We're leaving now, really early, so I can still see the glow and know the way.

I made Bunji and me two jam sandwiches. I took an apple, and I borrowed your yellow torch. I hope you don't mind. We might be gone all day but don't worry.

Alice

Bryn was now in the doorway. She handed him the note and then went to the high gable window that looked out over the mountains toward Sydney.

Alice could surely have seen Sydney last night. It was such a vast city that its glow could be seen for miles. Many, many miles.

And between here and that glow was a mountain range so vast, so overwhelming that it had taken years before the first settlers had found courage and endurance enough to cross it. The Great Dividing Range. The Blue Mountains. Most of it was impenetrable bushland, peaks, chasms, ravines, land so wild it had never been—could never be—built on.

If Alice had left before dawn... Dear God, she'd been gone for at least three hours. Maybe more. How long before dawn had she left? She'd have been walking in the dark.

She turned and saw Bryn staring at the note. His face was as ashen as hers felt.

'She'll have gone out the back,' she managed, but her voice was a thready croak. 'If she's following the glow... She can't possibly be trying to go by road—from here the road looks like it's going in the wrong direction.'

Then he was at the window beside her, staring out across the wilderness. A few hundred metres from the house the land fell away to a massive ravine. They could see the rock walls of the other side.

'She'll have tried to go around,' Kiara whispered. 'She'll never have tried to go straight across.'

'She doesn't know…' It was a groan. 'Hell. She heard what I said. Kiara, she heard. She thinks I don't want her.'

There was a moment's silence while last night's conversation replayed in both their heads, and if Bryn's face was ashen before then it was worse now.

'We'll find her.' She put her hand on his shoulder and then, because it seemed the only thing to do and she needed it as well, she tugged him tight and held. There was no time, but for these few seconds she took what she needed from that hug. And maybe he did as well, because when they parted his face was set.

'I'll go. There looks a path leading from the back…'

'There is,' she told him. 'But it peters out when the ground drops sharply at the edge of the ravine. There's a viewing platform Grandma built.'

'Then that's where I'll start. She might even have had the sense to stop there.'

'If she did then she'd be back now.'

'Then I'll go on. I have my phone. If I find her, I'll ring, but can you contact emergency services? Surely they'll come.' He was already heading for the door.

'Bryn. Stop!' She made her voice as firm as she could make it, and it came out almost as a yell. 'No. You can't make bad worse.'

He paused, looked back, looking ill. 'I have to go.'

'Do you know these mountains?'

'No, but...'

'And is your leg strong enough to climb? To move fast?'

There was a dreadful silence. His leg was healing. Every day it grew stronger, but he still walked with a perceptible limp.

'Kiara, I have to.' It came out a groan and she moved again to hug, a strong, all-encompassing hold where she held as much of him as she could.

'It'll be hard,' she managed, forcing back fear that made her own legs tremble. A little girl, out there alone... It felt appalling but she had to be sensible, and she had to make Bryn see sense as well. 'Bryn, you put your life on the line once before for Alice, but this isn't such a life and death situation. Sure, it's thick bush, but it's daylight now and she has Bunji. If she was on her own, she might try and climb down unsafe places to take a shortcut, but Bunji's limping, too, and she loves her.'

'So I'll find her...'

'You won't.' She put all the authority she could muster into her voice. 'Bryn, we'll have help in minutes. The first responders will be the team from the local fire brigade. They know this country like the back of their hands—they spend half their time fighting fires, and the rest of their time looking for lost hikers. I'll go with them because this area around here is my domain. Grandma taught me all about her country. I know every animal trail, every track within five kilometres. There's a sort of track leading down into the first ravine. If we can't find her within an hour, we'll send for back up. Because it's a child, we'll have rescue teams, helicopters, the works. But, Bryn, you need to stay here.'

'I can't.

'You must. There's every possibility she'll change her mind when it gets hard, and she'll come back. You need to be here.'

'I can't bear...'

'You have to bear,' she told him. 'We'll find her.'

He stared at her wildly, raked his hair and then swore and swore again. 'I do love her,' he said helplessly.

And at that, she drew his head down to hers and she kissed him. Hard, long, fiercely.

'I think you do,' she said simply when she finally pulled away. 'I've watched you with her. I think…maybe you love more than you believe you possibly can?'

What followed was a nightmare.

Waiting, waiting, waiting.

As Kiara promised, the fire brigade arrived in minutes. Serious men and women, dressed in bright yellow clothing and sturdy boots, with two-way radios, backpacks with ropes, medical supplies, compasses, maps.

It was obvious that Kiara was right—they did spend half their time searching for lost hikers. Their captain spoke seriously to Kiara and to Bryn, and a search was organised in minutes. The captain saw Bryn's limp at a glance, and she handed him a receiver.

'If I can leave this with you then I won't have to leave one of my team behind,' she told him, and he wondered if she said that to any relative desperate about a lost one. As if giving him a job could take his mind off worry. Ha!

'If we don't find her in an hour, we'll bring in further emergency services and choppers,' he was told. 'We have heat-seeking choppers if we need them—kangaroos mess with thermal imaging but our people are pretty good at discerning what's 'roo and what's kid. And you said she has a dog with her? That's a double image and it should help. We'll report back to you, and you'll hear everything that's going on. Don't worry, mate, we'll have her back to you in no time.'

They didn't.

Three hours later there was a lot more than one fire brigade team searching. Police were tracing every sighting of a kid and dog between here and the hospital—just in case Alice had changed her mind about the route. There were now ten official trucks lined up on the road outside. Emergency services had split into teams and were heading in from here. Others, Bryn gathered, were heading in from the other side of the ravine. As soon as word went out, local bushwalking groups, plus concerned locals, had abandoned their plans for the day and were splitting into more teams, heading down the ravine from a myriad entry points. There were two choppers overhead.

How hard could it be to find one kid and one dog?

There were more people in the kitchen now—they'd set it up as a field base for all services. He was still allowed to be on radio duty, but the set was taken over when orders had to be relayed.

He was going mad, and as the day wore on it grew worse. He tried to phone Kiara, but her phone seemed dead. 'There's no reception at the bottom of the ravines,' one of the emergency services people told him. 'She'll be with a team, and if she needs to contact you, she can use their radio.'

She didn't.

The day wore on. He couldn't eat. He couldn't think. As dusk fell and one of the local ladies—Donna had organised a food tent out at the front—put a hamburger in front of him he thought he might be ill.

Finally, someone handed him a radio. 'It's Miss Brail, sir. Wanting to talk.'

'Kiara.'

'Bryn.' Her voice was unsteady, and she tried again. 'Bryn.'

'No...'

'No news. But I'm at the bottom of the second ravine. The experts have done an assessment and they think, given the time frame, she may well have made it to here. The guys have camping gear. They dropped in supplies so we're staying put for the night. We figure...' Her voice cracked a little, but he heard a ragged breath and then she continued, more calmly. 'The thought is that she and Bunji are probably hunkered down behind a log, or somewhere that takes the edge from the wind. It's breezy down here and...and she'll be cold. Thank God it isn't raining. But we're searching again from dawn. Teams are searching across the top ridges and working their way down. We'll find her.'

'But tonight…'

'She has Bunji and she's a sensible kid. We'll find her.'

'Kiara…'

'See if you can get some sleep, Bryn.'

'As if I could.'

'I know. Bryn…'

'Kiara…'

'I know it won't work,' she whispered softly. 'But for what it's worth… know that I love you.'

And she disconnected.

How was a man to sleep after that? He didn't bother to get undressed, just lay in the dark and stared at the ceiling.

Somewhere out there was a little girl lost. A kid who needed him, who depended on him.

Somewhere out there was Kiara.

A woman who loved him.

He could do nothing.

And at some time in the small hours, when the lorikeets in the gums outside were starting their pre-dawn squawking, when the kookaburras' raucous laughter was once again starting to echo across the valley, he was hit by self-knowledge that almost blindsided him.

He'd been thinking, *Why not me who could be there searching?*

He'd been thinking, *Why not me who could be lost?*

He'd swap with each of them in a heartbeat, and with the first rays of dawn there it was. The sickening realisation that if he lost either of them, he'd lose part of himself.

They were part of him. How could he exist if he lost either? He'd do anything—*anything*—to keep them safe, happy…home.

Was that what was meant by love?

And as the sun slowly rose over the mountains, he knew that it was.

They found them at midday.

There was a crackle on the main receiver set. Bryn was sitting on the veranda steps, staring bleakly at nothing, and he heard someone answer. With so many search teams on the ground and in the air, the job of manning the main receiver had been handed to someone who was not…so emotionally involved? A cop. Sergeant Someone. There were so many people now, so many teams using this as a base.

But as the receiver cracked into life, everyone stilled as they always did. Straining to hear.

'Is that right?' And with that…was there exultation in the exclamation? He couldn't hear what was being said at the other end, but he could hear the cop. And unbelievingly he heard: 'Yeah?

Both safe? And the dog? Well, I'll be… Geezers, mate, you've made our day. Give us a minute while I go tell the dad.'

The dad. With strangers coming and going, introductions had been brief and relationships had been blurred. Maybe it had just been assumed that he was family?

But then the cop was out on the veranda, kneeling beside him, hand on his shoulder.

'They're safe, mate. All of them. Your missus was in the team that found them. They've been huddled in some sort of cave, scared to go on. It seems the kid had the sense to stay put when she realised she was lost. She's a bit scratched, hungry and thirsty and cold, but the guys said to tell you your missus is sitting on the ground with them, bawling her eyes out, hugging kid and dog like she'll never let go. We'll winch them all out as soon as we can but, mate, they're gonna be okay.'

There was a cheer around them, small at first as only those within earshot had heard, but then the ladies in the food tent outside heard, the teams changing shifts heard, the nosy parkers who'd edged into the front yard heard. The car horns went, the town heard, the roar of celebration rang out seemingly over the whole mountain range.

They were safe.

His family was safe. His little girl. His floppy-eared dog.

His Kiara. His love.

His life.

Two hours later Kiara was sitting in a chopper, going home. Alice, bundled in blankets, was huddled close. Bunji was wedged somewhere between them.

I'll take them, she thought as the chopper rose from the ravine where Alice and Bunji had spent an appalling thirty-six hours. If Bryn really doesn't want them then they'll stay with me. Whatever it takes… Sure, I'll be broke but if I give up Two Tails, get a job as a normal vet, I might be able to afford…

She was too tired to get past that thought. The chopper was sky-high now, clearing the massive eucalypts, heading home.

And then they were descending, to land on Birralong's football field. She could see clusters of people beneath them. A crowd to welcome them home.

There was a cloud of dust as the chopper settled and then a wait until the blades stopped rotating.

'We're not going to go to all this trouble to see you swiped with blades,' one of the crew told her, and his grin matched the relief in her own heart.

So many people who cared.

Maybe she *could* stay at Two Tails. Maybe the community might help. Maybe…

And then the rotors stilled, and silence fell. The doors were hauled back and people in green camouflage suits—army?—were helping them down.

She hardly saw them, because coming towards them…

Bryn.

Maybe someone had been holding him back because he emerged from the crowd like a runner released by the starter's gun. His limp simply wasn't there. Ten long strides, five interminable seconds, and he was with her.

She was set down by the chopper. The ground felt good under her feet. Great. Alice was being handed down after, and she went to take her into her arms.

But Bryn was before her. He was gathering Alice up, tight against his chest and then, in one purposeful move, he was gathering her in as well. Alice was sandwich-squeezed between them, and they were hugged as if he'd never let them go.

'Br… Bryn…' Alice quavered, as if the child was scared of a scolding.

'Oh, love,' Bryn said and then there was a silence while he hugged some more and struggled to find words to go on.

But then the words came…

'Maybe you'd better call me Dad,' Bryn told her, and he kissed the top of her head. 'I think… You've never had a dad, have you? Alice, I was so scared. I thought I'd lost you. Alice, what you heard me say was dumb. You and me…we're family. We're a team. And if it's okay with you, I'll never let you go.'

'D-Dad?' Alice said wonderingly and subsided into her blankets and was hugged some more.

Bunji was at their feet now. One of the team had set her down and she'd gone straight to them, part of the sandwich hug.

Part of family?

'Love?' Now Bryn was talking to her. To Kiara. She pulled back a little so she could see his face, and what she saw there… She went straight back into the hug. Back into where she most wanted to be in the world.

'You know what I said about marriage?' Bryn's voice was still unsteady.

'Mmff?' It was all she could say. Her face was muffled against his chest. People were milling around them now, people cheering, guys with cameras, journalists with notebooks ready. The noise was deafening but she heard only Bryn.

'I'd like to restart that conversation.'

'Mmm... Mmmff?'

And when he started talking it was as if they were completely alone, in their own world, a world where suddenly, magically, things were as right as they could possibly be.

'I got it wrong,' he told her, and his hold tightened even further. 'Kiara, you know all those dumb banners that people put up when they propose, saying *Love you for ever. Will you marry me?*—that sort of thing?'

'Um...yes?' Sort of. She was so confused but she managed to get the word out.

'I should have organised banners,' he told her. 'In fact, I still will. A million banners, my love, or at least as many banners as the sky can hold. If they're not real to the world, then they'll be real to us.'

'B...?'

'Banners,' he said, definitely and surely. And the banners will say only one thing. *Kiara, you have my heart.*'

They honeymooned in Queensland. If Bryn had ever thought of honeymoons he might have thought of the Bahamas, Hawaii, the Maldives, somewhere exotic and sensational. But when he and Kiara thought about it there seemed no option but to make their honeymoon a family affair. Which meant staying in Australia because…well, dog.

'Because this is what we are,' Bryn had said. 'From this day forth, we're a family, so let's start as we mean to go on. All in.'

Which meant Alice—of course. And then Bunji—naturally.

And then, when Kiara suggested they might like a little—just a little—time alone, Bryn had thought about Maureen, now almost recovered, back home with her beloved Jim, aching to be with Kiara and Alice but still a little shaky and frail. He'd tossed the idea to Kiara and she'd beamed. Thus they'd suggested Maureen and Jim might like to join them. A little Bunji and Alice dog-and-kid-minding might suit everyone.

Then they chose as their destination one of the magnificent islands bordering the Great Barrier Reef—one of the few where turtles didn't breed because…well…still dog. There was no way Bunji could be left behind.

They rented two beachfront villas, but then Kiara's friend Hazel said there was no way her best friend was being married without her. That meant hiring yet another villa, because Hazel would be travelling with her brand-new husband, Finn, and the pair intended to bring their precious, ready-made family as well.

And finally, on a stunning morning on a pristine, sun-soaked, tide-washed beach, Kiara Brail and Bryn Dalton were ready to be married.

Bryn stood on the sand before the celebrant, under the slightly wobbly arch of frangipani that Alice and Maureen and Jim had constructed with care and with love and with laughter. Behind him was Maureen, already sniffing and clutching her Jim, then Hazel's beloved Finn, Finn's daughter, Finn's granddaughter, and then a dog called Bunji and a dog called Ben.

Both rescue dogs.

But who had been rescued? Bryn thought, as he faced the celebrant, a wizened old surfer with a smile almost as broad as his face. It felt as if he had. And suddenly he was thinking of 'Two Tails.'

Two Tails had been named because of the phrase happy as a pup with two tails.

It had also been named for the combination of words: two tales—the story of before and after.

That pretty much summed up his life, he thought. This was his second tale—his happy ever after. His life felt as if it was starting right now.

He'd already made some huge changes. He'd keep his medicine because that was what he did, but it needed to be a part of his life, not the whole. He'd resigned from his teaching role, and he'd quit as head of department at Sydney Central. Amazingly his resignations had left him almost giddy with relief. There was no way they'd move Two Tails—it was perfect where it was, and he wanted to be part of it. With his money, with Hazel and Finn's support, it could be the best refuge ever.

The best home ever.

Where they could always be…well, happy as a pup with two tails.

Coming down the sandhills now were Alice and Hazel, bridesmaids in matching flowing sarongs, beaming like two conniving archangels whose plans had finally come to fruition. And here was Kiara. His bride.

She was simply dressed in soft white broderie anglaise—Alice had whispered to him that that was what the lacy confection was. It was sleeveless, clinging to her breasts, moulded to her waist and then flowing in soft folds to her bare feet and ankles. It was all white, bar for the tiny rainbow ribbons threaded through the lace. Her dusky curls were threaded with the same ribbon, and Alice had tucked frangipani into her hair.

'She's going to look bee-*yoo*-tiful,' she'd told Bryn and as the music swelled, as he turned to watch his bride approach, Bryn could only agree.

Mind, she would have looked beautiful in dungarees, he thought. She was his Kiara. His love. His life.

The music faded from the sound system the celebrant had set up, and the old surfer beamed at the pair of them. 'Are you ready to start?'

Was he ready? Kiara looked up at him, her eyes misty, and he thought his heart might well burst.

Two tales—before and after.

Happy as a dog with two tails.

Perfect.

He couldn't resist. He kissed the bride, right there and then, and then he nodded to the celebrant.

'We're ready,' he said, and Kiara smiled and smiled.

'Yes, we are,' she whispered, and kissed him back. 'We're ready for the rest of our lives.'

* * * * *

If you missed the previous story in the Two Tails Animal Refuge duet, then check out

The Vet's Unexpected Family
by Alison Roberts

If you enjoyed this story, check out these other great reads from Marion Lennox

Healing Her Brooding Island Hero
Falling for His Island Nurse
Mistletoe Kiss with the Heart Doctor

All available now!